# THE JINX
## of
# PAYROCK CANYON

*By*
TROY NESBIT

*Illustrated by*
URSULA KOERING

WHITMAN PUBLISHING COMPANY
RACINE, WISCONSIN

# CONTENTS

1. The Mysterious Parachute . . . . . . . . . . 9
2. The Changing Beaver . . . . . . . . . . . . 21
3. The Open Gate . . . . . . . . . . . . . . 31
4. Mountain Telepathy . . . . . . . . . . . . 40
5. Search for the Redheads . . . . . . . . . . 51
6. Marooned on a Ledge . . . . . . . . . . . 64
7. Skill and Nerve . . . . . . . . . . . . . 77
8. Danger in the Night . . . . . . . . . . . 89
9. The Man With the Box . . . . . . . . . . 96
10. Jinx of Payrock Canyon . . . . . . . . . . 107
11. Beaver Information . . . . . . . . . . . . 118
12. Trailing in the Tundra . . . . . . . . . . 128
13. Human Beaver Bait . . . . . . . . . . . . 143
14. The Blasted Cabin . . . . . . . . . . . . 154
15. "Crazy" . . . . . . . . . . . . . . . . 163
16. The Hunt Begins . . . . . . . . . . . . 176
17. In the Crevasse . . . . . . . . . . . . . 187
18. The Runaway Casualty . . . . . . . . . . 201
19. Reward Offered . . . . . . . . . . . . . 216
20. Into Devil's Crater . . . . . . . . . . . . 225
21. Clues to the Unexpected . . . . . . . . . . 245
22. Benzy, the Sleuth . . . . . . . . . . . . 264
23. "Hiking Hawkshaws" . . . . . . . . . . . 271

CHAPTER 1 ... The Mysterious Parachute

"Hey, lookit! Somebody just bailed out of that plane!" Jason Himrod yelled excitedly to Doc. Both boys reined in their horses and watched the parachute open, then glide out of sight over the rim of the cliff just above them.

"Gee, I bet something's wrong," Doc said. "Engine trouble, maybe." The plane was gone now, hidden from sight by the cliff. "Let's get up there and see what's going on."

Jay and Doc swung out of their saddles, tied the horses, then listened. They could not hear the plane's engine any longer. Maybe it had crashed. Maybe the roar of the waterfall just ahead of them drowned out the sound.

"Come on!" Jay said. "There used to be a trail up the

right end of the cliff. Let's hurry."

Doc groaned. He wanted to find out about the parachute and the plane. But he hated to go anywhere that his horse couldn't take him. Jay felt a flash of amused satisfaction. At last something had made Doc Martin do a little hiking. Jay himself had always loved climbing in this part of the high Colorado Rockies above the ghost town of Payrock in which he had spent all of his fifteen years.

Jay's long, hard-muscled legs took him nimbly up the steep trail. Behind him ran Benzy, his small yellow dog.

"There's something new here," Jay shouted back down to Doc when he reached the top of the fifty-foot cliff.

In front of him stretched a wire-mesh fence with metal posts. It ran from the bank of the stream high up along the almost perpendicular shoulder of the mountain. A similar wire fence stood on the opposite side of the stream. Somebody had closed off the mouth of the canyon down which the stream ran. As Jay climbed over the barrier, he saw something else new—a pond that hadn't been there when he last visited the place about four years ago.

"Beavers been at work," Doc panted as he caught up

with Jay. "Look at the dam they made."

But Jay's eyes traveled up from the beaver pond. There was the airplane again. It had apparently circled and come back. The falls drowned out the sound of its engine, so they hadn't noticed its approach. It was flying low and they could see that its right door had been removed. Suddenly a man behind the pilot pushed something out of the cockpit. For the second time a parachute snapped open and came slowly toward earth with a curious pendulum-like motion. Clearly there was no man in the harness of the chute—just some sort of bundle.

The bundle touched the ground and the parachute slumped near it. The boys ran, stumbling over the rough, marshy earth and dodging through clumps of brush that scratched roughly at their old blue jeans. Both of them ignored Benzy, who barked helplessly from the far side of the close-meshed wide fence. He couldn't get through, and with his stubby little legs he was no jumper.

When the boys reached the parachute, they found that its burden consisted only of a queer-looking box about the size of a fat suitcase—and an empty box, at that! Round holes were bored at intervals in the heavy wood. Ropes from the parachute ran through it and around it.

Across the bottom were great, heavy rubber bands.

"What kind of contraption is that!" Doc said in surprise.

Jay looked up at the plane, as if seeking an explanation. It had climbed steeply after dropping the parachute and was now headed off to the northeast, over the high ridge that made one wall of the U-shaped canyon.

"What about the first chute we saw?" Jay wondered. "The fellow that bailed out must be around here someplace."

The boys swung their eyes over the cluttered land around the beaver pond. They saw nothing but ragged brush, stumps left where beavers had felled aspen trees, and the senseless pattern made by aspen trunks which the little animals had chewed down but had been unable to drag to the pond.

Then, clambering through this tangle, they saw a man coming toward them.

"There he is!" Jay burst out excitedly.

The man waved.

"Why, that looks like Van!" Doc exclaimed.

Sure enough, it was Ovando Hollister. Both the boys knew him well. Hollister worked for the Colorado Game and Fish Department, and Doc had often got information from him about the wild animals he loved to study when he was out riding range in high mountain cattle country.

"Hey, Van, what's going on? Did you just jump out of that plane?" Doc called.

"Naw." Van grinned "That was two other guys."

"Quit kidding," Jay protested.

"Didn't you see the one that came down in this chute here?" Van asked.

"Aw, go on," said Doc.

"There he is now." Van pointed to the pond.

The boys saw nothing but a growing V-shaped ripple in the surface of the water.

"That's just a beaver," Jay observed with confidence.

"Not *just* a beaver," Van corrected him. "A black beaver, and he climbed out of this box."

"I suppose a cute little white beaver was piloting that plane," Jay came back at him.

"You mean that beaver dropped out of that plane in that box?" Doc asked incredulously.

"That's right," said Van. "We're trying an experiment in transplanting."

And then he went on to explain. The Fish and Game

Department often moved beavers from one place to another. They called it transplanting. First Van used special traps and caught the beavers alive in places where there were too many of them. Then he took these four-legged engineers and let them out along streams where they could build dams that would store up water and prevent floods. Every year Van and the trappers who worked with him harvested thousands of the beavers. That is, they killed them and skinned them. Then the state sold the pelts on the fur market and used the money for protecting other wild life.

Usually, Van explained, he and the others carried live beavers in cages on horseback. But today they were experimenting with parachutes. It was a lot quicker and easier to transplant from an airplane.

"I knew beavers were smart, but I didn't know they were smart enough to open up a box and get out," said Doc.

"It's simple. Look," Van said, lifting the box by the ropes that held it to the chute. "The pressure of the ropes on the sides of the box holds it shut while it's in the air. But when the box hits the ground, the pressure goes off. Then the strips of rubber inner tubing across the bottom and up the sides of the box start to work. They work like a spring hinge. They pull the box open automatically so that Mr. Beaver can hop out. We always drop a Mrs. Beaver, too, so they can set up housekeeping," he added.

"What's that you said about black ones?" Doc asked.

"There are only a few black beaver in this state," Van answered. "Their pelts bring twice as much as the ordinary brown kind, so we're trying to find a way of increasing the number of black ones. We want to raise a whole crop of them in this canyon and then start spreading them over the state."

"Is that why you've got a fence by the waterfall?" Doc asked.

"Yep," Van answered. "They can't go downstream because of the fence and the waterfall. They can't take off cross-country and move someplace else, because the sides of the canyon are too steep and too high. Theoretically, when a beaver's here he stays here."

"How many have you got in the canyon now?" Doc asked.

"Just two pair," Van answered, "the ones we brought in today and a pair we dropped farther up the canyon yesterday. We ought to have a lot more than that, but something screwy happened to the others we put in every year for the last three years."

"Did they die off?" Doc asked.

"No, we put in black ones, but when we checked up on them the next year, they'd all turned brown. And that ain't according to nature."

"What do you mean?" Jay asked curiously.

"Well, you might call it a mystery or a jinx. We put in full-grown black ones in August, but by the next March, they've all turned brown."

"Maybe there's something in the water," Jay suggested.

"Maybe," Van answered. "But I've been talking to those scientific fellows down at the college, and they say it just ain't possible. All they say is black beavers can't turn brown. They got me thinking I'm half nuts, because I've put in black ones and got out brown ones three years running."

"Say," Doc exclaimed, "do you suppose it's the same thing that's turning a lot of the aspen trees brown?" He looked along the slope of the canyon. Here and there were groves where stiff, dead leaves hung from the branches instead of the usual shimmery green. "It's happening in

spots like these all through the hills."

"Grandma says it might be poison in the air from the atom bomb blasts," Jay said. "I bet atoms *could* turn the trees and the beavers brown."

"I dunno," said Van. "But the place sure seems to be jinxed. I'm going to try it just this once more, and if it doesn't work, I give up."

"It all sounds nuts to me," Jay said. "I bet the black ones moved out and brown ones moved in."

"How could they get out?" Van said, pointing meaningfully at the impassable barriers made by the canyon walls on three sides and to the fence and waterfall on the fourth. "But this year I can keep track of 'em. I've put numbered metal clips in the ears of the black ones that just came in by plane."

"Say, that gives me an idea," Jay said. "Doc and I do a lot of riding near this place, looking after his dad's cattle. If those beaver tags are big enough to see, we can keep an eye on them for you."

"Have you turned cowpuncher, too?" Van asked Jay. "Isn't your grandma getting a little too old to handle the Payrock store all by herself?"

"Oh, I work in the store all right," Jay answered. "But

this year Mr. Martin hired me to ride range with Doc on the days Grandma doesn't need me."

Grandma Himrod had taken care of Jay ever since the death of both his parents when he was a baby. She always said he wasn't cut out for store work, and she hated to keep him indoors. But she was nearly eighty years old now, and with her stiff old joints she couldn't handle the cartons of canned goods any more. In a way, it was lucky that only a dozen people lived in Payrock during the winters now, when Jay had to be away at school. Grandma could take care of the store herself, with Jay doing the heavy chores on week ends.

Jay's muscles always did the pushing and pulling that was asked of them, but—winter or summer—as he worked, at least half of his mind was on the mountains where he loved to climb. This year there had been much less time for hiking than ever before. Jay needed the money Mr. Martin paid him for helping Doc to look after the cattle.

Van Hollister turned to Doc. "Your father must be running a lot of steers on the range if he needs extra help."

"No," Doc answered. "We've just been having more trouble with them than usual."

"Looks like there's a kind of general jinx around here," Van commented. He began to fold up the parachute. "Would you fellows lug this and the box down to the foot of the cliff? I'll bring the other one. I got a pack horse waiting there."

"I guess we were so interested in the plane and the chutes that we didn't notice your horses," Jay said. "We sure thought there was going to be a crash."

## CHAPTER 2 ... The Changing Beaver

"Uh-oh! Looks like we're in trouble again," Jay said to Doc as they approached the wire fence at the mouth of the canyon. The two boys were carrying the beaver box and parachute. Doc looked ahead. There stood Benzy, Jay's little yellow dog, waiting for them on the other side of the fence. In his mouth he held a black cap, the kind that miners wear when they are at work.

Benzy's long yellow tail was waving a vigorous wigwag of delight and achievement.

"You thieving, low-down, pedigreed Indian gopher hound," Jay said affectionately. "I'll teach you to keep on stealing. I'm sick and tired of finding out who belongs to the loot you drag in."

"Well, at least we don't have to go very far to find the owner of that cap he has there," said Doc. "I'd know that thing anywhere. It's Ashy's."

"I'd just as soon not tangle with the old crosspatch," Jay said, screwing up his lean, tanned face.

The boys heaved the parachute and box over the fence, and after they had swung themselves over, Jay recovered the cap.

"How do you suppose this mooching pooch got into the habit of stealing things wherever he goes?" Jay said. "I wish I had a dollar for every time Grandma has made me hike around Payrock returning a shoe or a market bag or some kid's doll that Benzy picked up."

"Animals get funny habits," said Doc. "Wild ones do queer things, too. No two of them are alike. And it's the same with people. Now look at you. You claim you like to hike and climb mountains and such nonsense. Anybody in his right mind knows that kind of work is for horses— not intelligent human beings."

Jay laughed. "I wonder where Ashy is. He and that cap can't be far apart."

Since both his hands were needed to help carry the box, he set the black cap on top of the battered Stetson hat he wore on his own head.

In a minute Van joined them, and the three moved

through the thick aspens to the place where Van's horses were tethered. There in a little clearing, stretched out on the ground with his bare head against a rucksack for a pillow, lay a white-bearded old man.

"I knew Ashy would be around," Jay said uneasily.

At the sound of the boy's voice, the old man opened his eyes. He stared at the approaching group in silence. Even stretched out on the ground, he had a prickly, barbed-wire look about him. Then he spied the hat and cap on Jay's head and glanced at the ground at his side in surprise.

"What do you think you're up to, young man?" he said sternly, sitting bolt upright.

It had never occurred to Jay or Doc to play a trick on Ashy. He just wasn't the sort of person you joked with. Now it was clear he thought Jay had swiped the cap, and the boys were a little flustered. They knew the old man wouldn't see any humor in the pilfering habits of Jay's underslung dog.

A little shamefaced, Jay handed him the cap and mumbled that Benzy had picked it up and they were just returning it. Ashy gave them a formidable grunt and turned to Van.

"I was just going home from the store when I saw that-there airplane," he said. "Found your horses here and figured you'd be back soon. Decided to rest awhile and get the news. What's going on, anyway?"

The old man clearly assumed that he had a right to an explanation. As Van talked, Jay studied the wiry, white-bearded figure. Ashy had been living in a cabin at the mouth of the Acorn Mine for longer than most people could even remember. To Jay he seemed as much a part of the mountains as the deep, changeless canyons that had been dug out by glaciers ages ago.

Grandma had told Jay a lot about Ashy and the early days when Payrock was a booming silver- and gold-mining camp. Ashy had appeared there as a lone, self-reliant boy of fifteen or sixteen who made his living as a mule-skinner. Grandma used to watch him through the store window as he drove teams of four or six, pulling heavy ore wagons from the mines to the reducing mills in Payrock. Then, when the boom ended in the early nineteen-hundreds, Ashy had clung on, living near the Acorn Mine. The mine had once produced ore. But, when the price of precious metal fell, its owner went out of business. He owed Ashy quite a large amount of money at the time, so he deeded him the mine in payment.

In all the years since then, Ashy had lived in hope that the price of ore would go up and he would become a rich man. Meantime, he made a living mainly by collecting old iron from abandoned mines and mills and selling it for junk. In recent years, he had not even kept mules or horses. He carried loads of small metal scraps in his rucksack, which was as much a part of him as his cap. Because he lived in the high mountains all year round, he picked up a small wage here and there as caretaker for summer cabins and camps.

The spry old man loved walking endlessly, and he often furnished Van with valuable tips and information about the wildlife he saw in the area. When Van had finished telling about the black beavers, Ashy grunted. He had no explanation for their change in color either. But, like the boys, he volunteered to keep an eye on the new arrivals.

"I'll tell you something else that needs looking at, too," Ashy said to Van. "That's the mountain sheep up on the ridges. Last week I found a dead ewe, and this morning I found another. I could see they didn't die of old age or the scab disease that used to get them years ago. Do you reckon they could have been poisoned?"

"You don't say!" Van exclaimed. "Whereabouts? I'd like to get the stuff out of their stomachs so I can have it tested."

"One carcass is just below Granny's Wart on the side of Comanche Peak. Tell you what. I was fixing to go and finish picking up a lot of old bolts at the Molly Q Mine one of these days. I might as well go tomorrow, and I can get those stomachs for you at the same time, if a coyote or a bear hasn't already got them. It'd be a shame if that bunch of bighorns got killed off."

This was an offer of help that Van readily accepted. He had his hands full these August days with his beaver work. Late summer was the best season for transplanting beaver, because there was time enough left before winter for the animals to build new dams and lodges, but there wasn't time enough for them to take off across country in search of their former homes. Van had actually known them to travel thirty or forty miles back home, after he had transplanted them early in the summer. He wanted his beaver to stay just where he put them, so they would build dams and help prevent spring floods.

"I appreciate that," Van told Ashy. "You bring the

sheep stomachs to Grandma Himrod's store and I'll pick them up and take 'em to the laboratory. Better put them in a lard pail with a tight lid, so you won't drive Grandma's customers away. Right, Jay?"

"And so this thieving hound of mine can't get at them," Jay added. "I expect to get sent to jail any day because he's robbed the U. S. mail."

"I wouldn't keep a dog like that," Ashy grumbled.

Jay said nothing. He had learned long ago that there was no way of getting any grownup to understand how he felt about his mischievous, ill-shaped pet.

The boys helped lash the beaver boxes to the pack-saddle on one of Van's horses. Without even saying good-by, Ashy left them and headed off southward toward his cabin.

"We'll ride with you as far as Lucky Lake, Van. Then we have to go up the south fork of the creek," Doc announced.

"That's a mighty pretty buckskin you're riding," Van said to Doc, as the boys brought their horses from the foot of the cliff. "You don't see many with the line-back marking in this part of the state. Where'd you get him?"

"Dad picked him up when he went down south to the

San Luis Valley to buy some steers last year," Doc answered. "He says that any horse with a black line like this right down the middle of its back is sure to be a good mountain pony. It's descended straight from the mustangs that used to roam wild all over the Southwest. Buck is as tough as rawhide and smart."

Doc was proud of his sturdy little horse. He liked the way the soft buckskin coloring made a perfect blend with the weathered tan of his saddle. The sharp, black line running from the mane along the spine to the black tail seemed a special badge of honor. And he was never happier than when he felt beneath him the rhythmic heave of the animal's strong haunches.

Jay rode a tall sorrel mare named Maude who belonged to Doc's father. At a gallop on a fairly level stretch of mountain road, she could outdistance Buck. But it wasn't very often that the boys kept to the roads. For the most part they scoured through fallen timber or followed the rough ridges above timberline, as they kept an eye on the Martin cattle. Ever since he was a little kid, Doc had been riding in this summer range country with his father. Now Doc was able to do most of the riding, while Mr. Martin looked after his cattle-feeding lot down on the plains.

As the horses picked their way over the narrow trail toward Lucky Lake, the three riders were silent for some time. Then Jay said suddenly, "I can't figure out about those mountain sheep. There's not a single poisonous plant I've ever heard about that grows above timberline. Who in the world would want to poison mountain sheep on purpose?"

"I can't figure it either," Van replied. "In the old days, dumb cattlemen put out poison for bears, but they used poison meat. Anyway, I don't know any dumb ranchers around here now." And he winked at Doc.

Jay went on thinking out loud. "If Grandma is right that atomic dust has poisoned a lot of the trees, maybe the sheep ate grass that was poisoned by atoms, too."

"Maybe there was poison in the chemicals that those cloud seeders dropped up here when they tried to make rain last spring," Doc suggested.

Van shrugged. "The laboratory will tell us if it's poison, and when we know that we can try to get rid of it."

"Looks as if the sheep are jinxed as well as the beavers and my dad's cattle," Doc said. "I wonder if there could be any connection."

## CHAPTER 3 ... The Open Gate

Jay and Doc reined in their horses and looked about with amazement at the sight in front of them. After leaving Van, they had ridden up the south fork of Payrock Creek as far as the road near Little Blue Lake. Then they had turned into the grounds of Camp Wapiti, a boys' camp built along the lake shore. This was the place near which some Martin cattle had caused trouble a few days before.

Jay's reason for wanting to ride through the camp itself wasn't altogether a noble one. Wapiti was run by Texans, and it was filled with Texas boys. Maybe there would be a chance to poke up a little interest in the traditional feud between Colorado boys and boys from the state they considered a rival. But when Jay saw what lay ahead, he forgot all his plans for making wisecracks about the Lone Star State.

31

Two of the big olive-drab tents that camp children slept in were tumbled in shapeless heaps on their wooden platforms. A clothesline full of bathing suits and beach robes had been torn down and dragged through the dirt. The Texas boys, most of them little shavers, were in an excited huddle on the broad plank steps that led up to their log dining-hall.

In the far corner of the camp, Jay and Doc saw the obvious cause of the confusion. There, about twenty steers, all with Mr. Martin's Circle M brand, were snorting and swinging their big, stupid heads anxiously. The cattle had plainly stampeded through the camp.

An angry counselor called, "Hey, aren't you the Martin boy?" Doc grunted an admission, and the counselor went on, "Will you-all please get your ornery critters out of here?"

"How did they get in?" Doc wanted to know. There was a new barbed-wire fence all around the camp to prevent exactly this from happening.

"We haven't had time to look around, but they're sure here. Come on, now, get 'em out so we can see what damage they've done."

This wasn't at all the kind of thing the boys had looked

forward to. The Texans obviously had the upper hand.
Jay grinned a little, thinking that the best he could do
now was to show that Colorado boys could ride and handle
cattle along with the best of them on the Texas ranges.
Without a word, Jay spurred Maude up the hill a little
way to the place where he knew a gate had been built
into the fence.

The gate was ingeniously rigged so that it swung itself
shut, even if youngsters from the camp went through and
forgot to close it. A rock weight on a pulley worked it
automatically. But now it stood wide open. And Jay saw
that the rock weight was gone. A loose rope merely dangled
uselessly.

Jay wheeled his horse and swung back down the hill.
"The gate's open," he called to the counselor. "That's
how the steers got in. Some of your kids must have untied
the rock weight." Now he felt considerably cheered up.
The camp couldn't blame the trouble on Doc or him or
even on the Circle M steers.

Moving the excited cattle slowly and making a wide
circle away from the tents, Jay and Doc got the animals
through the gate. A couple of counselors and the camp
manager followed, and a chattering crew of barelegged

little boys swarmed behind them.

All the camp boys were shouting at once and offering proof that they couldn't have removed the stone that kept the gate closed. As the counselors used their best Boy Scout knots to tie the rope back into working position around the stone, Benzy wormed his way into the circle of bare legs. He wagged his tail furiously by way of calling attention to his latest find. In his mouth he held a blue bandanna handkerchief.

"Looks like Benzy's got something," Jay said. "Who does this bandanna belong to?" The person who had been monkeying around with the gate must have dropped his bandanna. So they could find out in a hurry which was the culprit.

A counselor gave a quick look and snapped, "That doesn't belong to anyone here. We all have red bandannas, and besides the boys have name-tapes sewed into all their things. This one's blue and doesn't have any name-tape."

"One thing's sure. It hasn't been out here very long. Hasn't even been rained on," Jay said. But he felt a little annoyed that his clue was useless. He was beginning to think that the camp kids really had not opened the gate. He was puzzled by another thing. Why had the cattle

stampeded through the gate?

The natural thing would be for them to wander slowly through—and certainly the steers would keep away from the tents where so many campers were running around making a racket.

"Doc," Jay said, "those steers sure must have been spooked by something."

"Do you suppose a mountain lion got after them?" asked one of the pair of long-legged, red-haired twins in the group.

"Or a bear?" the other twin added hopefully.

Doc laughed. "There are no grizzlies around here," he said with quiet authority. "No brown bear or mountain lion would bother a bunch of full-grown steers—not at this time of year, certainly. They have a lot easier ways of getting a meal in the summertime."

"I think some*body* spooked them," said Jay. But he looked down hopelessly at the tangle of men's and boys' footprints all around. If a human being had been up to some sort of mischief, there was no chance of finding his tracks now.

"*I* think there's something wrong with your cattle," said the same bossy counselor who had first spoken to

Doc. "The other day, as I told your father," he went on sternly, "my boys were having a steak-fry up by Bell's Mill and suddenly a bunch of Circle M steers charged right out of the timber toward our fire. Luckily they turned when they saw the fire and the children. That's unnatural behavior in this kind of animal. But I won't have my boys frightened this way again."

Jay knew there was something strange about the whole thing, but all he could think of saying was, "Well, you explain it to the cattle. Mr. Martin's got a permit to run them on this range."

Jay glanced toward Doc who was now listening to an unpleasant speech from the camp manager. A sudden idea occurred to Jay and he called out, "Hey, do you suppose it could have been the airplane that spooked the cattle?"

"What airplane?" asked the red-headed twins, both at once. "We didn't see any plane."

Amused, Jay said, "Didn't you see the parachutes? No, I guess you couldn't. They were across the ridge from here."

Immediately the redheads clamored for an explanation, and Jay told them briefly about the beavers. The counselor was interested, too, and he began to soften up a little. He asked Jay for details, saying he might lead the children on a hike over there some day.

"I don't know if the Game and Fish people would want a crowd of kids in there with new beavers that have just been transplanted," Jay said doubtfully. He wished now that he hadn't brought the subject up. "You better call the office down in Fremont before you go monkeying around."

Jay was a little worried. Maybe these wild Texas kids would do something to spoil the experiment, and then he would be to blame for having told them.

"Let's get going, Jay," Doc called. He wanted to light out, before the camp manager grew any more disagreeable. The argument was something his father would have to settle anyway. Meantime, he wanted to shove the cattle away from the camp, up to a good alpine meadow they apparently had not discovered near timberline.

As the two boys rode slowly up the wooded slope behind the steers, Doc said, "I can't figure it. It certainly wasn't the plane that spooked the critters. The manager said definitely it didn't fly over here. Somebody must be stampeding the cattle. But who would want to scare those kids twice in a week, anyway?"

"Jinx, I guess," Jay said glumly. "I sure hope I didn't put some more jinx on Van's beavers, too." He told Doc about his conversation with the counselor and the red-headed kids. "They were all too darn interested, and the kids wanted to start right out to 'case the joint,' they said. Do you think that a bunch of crazy little Texas Rangers could scare the beavers out of building houses?"

"I don't know," Doc replied. "Looks like almost anything could happen around here."

## CHAPTER 4 ... Mountain Telepathy

Jay took a bottle of soda pop out of the old-fashioned kitchen refrigerator in Grandma Himrod's store. "That's the last cold one, folks," he called out happily to the customers in general. Now maybe he wouldn't have to keep opening and slamming the refrigerator door.

It seemed to Jay that his grandmother's store was more crowded than it had ever been before. Customers had run him ragged this afternoon asking for nickel bars of candy and bottles of pop. For the last hour he hadn't been able to get started with the big job of opening new cases of canned goods and restocking the shelves. He knew he had to get it all done if he wanted to have tomorrow off for a hike he was planning to take.

The unusually brisk trade was caused by a delay in the arrival of the mail truck. Every afternoon at about three o'clock, the truck was supposed to come up the steep mountain road from the town of Fremont down on the plains. About three-thirty, people from all over the area around Payrock wandered in to get their mail. The post office and Grandma's store were side by side in an old frame building that had been a station on the narrow-gauge railroad fifty years ago. Naturally, when the mail was late, people drifted down the high platform and into the store, since there was nothing to do in the post office.

Now a tall, burly man dressed in expensive dude ranch clothes came in off the platform where he had been pacing impatiently back and forth. "I'm going to phone the post office in Fremont and see what's happened to that mail truck," he announced. "Four-thirty! It's outrageous." He tossed a twenty-dollar bill down on the counter where Grandma Himrod sat near an old-fashioned cash register. "Will you give me change, so I can use the phone?"

Grandma Himrod adjusted her glasses on her wrinkled, pink face. Her age-stiffened hands opened the cash drawer.

"I'm sorry, Mr. George, I've got plenty of bills, but

no small silver. Seems like everybody has cleaned me out, making change for candy and soda pop this afternoon."

After considerable spluttering, the big man found a customer who could change his bill. Then he went to the phone and jiggled the receiver hook up and down. The operator apparently didn't answer. He jiggled some more. Then he slammed the receiver down and growled, "Phone's dead."

A voice from the doorway said, "I don't wonder." People turned to look, although everyone knew who had spoken.

"Hello, Ashy," Grandma said, as the bearded face of the spry, angular old man appeared.

"Hello, Ashforth," said the man called Mr. George. "You don't wonder what?"

"That the phone's out," Ashy replied. "As I came down the mountain I saw some mighty mean-looking thunderheads over the lower part of the canyon. There was probably a flash flood that washed some poles out and pulled the lines down."

"That's probably why the mail truck hasn't come, too," said Grandma. "You know, Ashy, I never can get used to people worrying over their mail. When you and I were young up here, we just took it when it came—every two or three or four days." Grandma interrupted herself to look up at a large figure entering the door. Then with a twinkle in her eye she threw up her hands and said, "I didn't do it, Sheriff, honest I didn't."

The big man in the doorway grinned, took off his Stetson hat, rubbed his head, and put the hat back on. "Hiyah, Grandma, Jay, Ashy," he said. He went on around the room calling everybody by name till he came to the man who had tried to make the telephone call.

"Don't *you* know Mr. George, Sheriff?" asked Grandma. "He's the one that bought the old Sky-High Ranch."

"I've never had the pleasure," he said.

Mr. George held out his hand to the sheriff. "Jerrold George the Third. And your name, sir?"

"Bert McKenney," the sheriff answered. The two big men shook hands.

"Give me an orange pop, Jay," the sheriff said.

"It won't be cold," Jay warned him.

"If it's wet, that's all I care," said the sheriff, producing a dime. "I had to drive the long way around getting here. I suppose you know the Seven Mile Bridge is out. There was a flash flood down the canyon a while ago. In case you didn't know, your phone's dead, too."

"We just found out about the phone," said Grandma, "but what's so important around here that you had to come yourself right now?"

The sheriff took a leisurely swig of warm pop. "Oh, the usual," he answered. "A certain number of kids have to get lost in the hills every summer, and the quota's not full yet. Got a call from that Wapiti camp just before the phone line washed out. Seems a pair of red-headed twins disappeared early this morning, and a couple of hours ago the camp began to get worried. I said I'd get together some searchers. Though I might pick up a few here at Payrock and start looking. The Search and Rescue Squad fellows will be up here with all their equipment in an hour or so."

This news filled Jay with acute misery. His work in the store wasn't nearly done, and the search would be starting right now. He was so eager to go along that he blurted out, "Grandma, can I go, and finish my work tomorrow?"

"Sure," the old lady answered, almost crossly. "Kids are more important than groceries."

Jay dashed through the door at the back of the store

which led to the part of the old railroad station where
he and Grandma lived. In his own room, he fumbled for
a key in the pocket of his jeans and hastily opened a padlock on a box that hung like a cupboard on one wall.
Inside of the box was an old-fashioned telephone with
a crank at one side. Jay whirled the crank furiously. Then
he whirled it again. This was Jay's end of the private
telephone line that he and Doc had rigged up between
their homes. Long ago the phone company had somehow
forgotten to remove the instruments from abandoned mine
buildings nearby. The boys had appropriated them and
now used them as a secret means of communication. No
grownups had been specifically let in on the deal. But
the Martins and Grandma Himrod were pretty sure they
knew the meaning of the ringing bells in the boys' rooms.

Jay just hoped that Doc was in his home now. The
Martin house was more than a half-mile away by a winding
road, but only about two hundreds yards away straight up
a very steep hill and over the top. It would take Doc
less than a minute to race down the hill and join the
rescue party—if Jay could reach him.

Doc *was* at home, and Jay breathlessly told him the
story the sheriff had given him.

"Don't let them get away," Doc shouted into his end of the phone. "I'll be right down!"

He was. Almost as soon as Jay got back into the store, he could hear Doc's feet thundering on the platform outside. The screen door slammed open and Doc burst in, panting a little from his run down the steep slope.

"Hi, Bert," he said to the sheriff. "I know exactly where those red-headed twins are. I'll go along and show you."

"Yeah?" the sheriff drawled in his usual slow way. Then his eyes focused on Doc with sudden intensity. "Hey, you weren't here when I told about the kids. How do you know so much about 'em?"

Doc and Jay looked at each other. "It's telepathy, sir," Jay said innocently.

"Telepathy?" Mr. George blustered.

"Yes, sir," said Jay. "I just have to go off by myself and concentrate. And, every time, Doc sort of picks up my brain waves."

The sheriff gave a quick look at Grandma, who was smiling, then he turned back to Jay. "Do *you* think you know where those Texas kids are, too?"

"I don't *think*. I'm certain," Jay said. "Tell him, Doc."

Everybody looked at Doc, who closed his eyes, put his

hands on his round face, and said slowly, as if he were hypnotized: "Those boys are near the Game and Fish experimental beaver preserve on the Middle Fork of Payrock Creek. The only thing I'm not sure of is whether they are lost in the woods or stuck on a cliff somewhere near there."

The sheriff saw that the boys knew something he didn't know, but he was the kind of man who never liked to admit ignorance. "First time I ever met anybody who could read my mind," he said. "That's pretty rough country up there. I guess I'd better get a few more volunteers to beat through the woods. If we find the kids before the Search and Rescue Squad arrives, no harm done."

The sheriff looked around the room. "Ashy, will you go?" he asked.

"I suppose so," Ashy said with irritation. "These summer campers are more trouble than they're worth."

"Mr. George?" the sheriff went on.

Jerrold George III looked down significantly at the sporty sandals on his feet. "I'm afraid I haven't got the right shoes for it," he said. "Very sorry."

Nobody else in the store could go right away.

"Guess I'll have to scare up somebody else from around

town here," the sheriff said. He pushed the screen door
open to go out, and Benzy's low, squirming body almost
tripped him up. Banging along on the floor between the
dog's front paws was a big hiking boot.

Suddenly Mr. George made a lunge for Benzy, but
Benzy was too quick. He leaped out of reach and dragged
the boot over to Jay, then dropped it. He looked up at his
master as if for approval.

Grandma was annoyed. "Sheriff, now's your chance,"
she said. "Put handcuffs on that thief and take him with
you to the lockup."

Without a word, Jay picked up the boot and handed it
to Mr. George. Then, as an afterthought, he said, "Nice,
comfortable-looking boot for hiking."

Mr. George seized the boot, stalked out, and tossed it
into the open rear end of his blue station wagon which
was backed up to the platform.

People in the store moved toward the doorway to watch.
They grinned at each other as the big man started his motor
and drove off with a red face.

The sheriff strode toward his own car. Jay nudged Doc.
"That was sure a good hunch you had about those redheads," he said. "I'm positive they streaked off to see the

black beavers the first chance they would get."

"Bert McKenney is kind of a show-off, isn't he?" Doc observed. "He tried to let on in front of everybody that he knew where the kids might have gone. Why, I betcha even the camp counselors don't know."

Suddenly a low, loud moan rose to a piercing shriek outside the door. "Land o' Goshen!" Grandma exclaimed. "Bert sure was right when he said he'd *scare* up some volunteers."

In no time at all, summer people came running out of the white frame houses scattered along the town's three steep streets. As they ran toward the sheriff's car, his siren kept up its weird wail.

## CHAPTER 5 ... Search for the Redheads

"I wish I had my horse," Doc moaned good-naturedly as he and the sheriff strode along trying to keep up with Jay.

They had left the sheriff's car at the end of the road by Lucky Lake. Now they were winding up the familiar trail toward the beaver preserve. The trail was steep, and Doc and the sheriff were both breathing heavily. Ahead of them, they could see Jay's long legs which seemed to move as if the only effort in each stride was an effort to keep from going faster.

"That pal of yours is part mountain goat," the sheriff commented in a way that at once showed respect for Jay and a fellow-feeling for Doc. "I guess you and I both have spent more time in a saddle than we have afoot. Still, it wouldn't be any use for us to have horses up here tonight. We may have a lot of scrambling to do through country that would stop a horse."

"Guess you're right," Doc panted.

"Let's *blow*!" Jay shouted. Every few hundred yards he sounded out his call, the way he had heard professional guides call to tourists. It was a signal to stop and take a breather. Jay waited till Doc and the sheriff caught up with him. He gave them a few moments' rest, then bellowed as if he had fifty people spread out behind him, "Let's *go*!"

"Aw, come on!" Doc protested. "You get three times as much rest as we do, and you don't need any of it. Give us a break."

" 'There's work to be done and throats to be cut,' " Jay quoted and dramatically waved them onward. "My English teacher says that's from Shakespeare."

"At least there's a good strong lecture to give," the sheriff said. "From what the manager at the camp said, those two kids just broke regulations and sneaked off without telling a living soul where they were headed. Young 'uns can get in serious trouble that way, and then sometimes the rescuers get hurt besides. It's no good to joke with these mountains."

The long evening shadows already filled the canyon bottom, and both boys were quite willing to agree that the country around them was no place to play irresponsible pranks. Up high ahead of them the jagged gray ridge of the Continental Divide was hacking away at the setting sun. White patches of snow on the top of Elizabeth Glacier, which was just in sight, reminded them what a cold place the mountains could be. Already chill air from the peaks was crowding down among the aspens and the lodgepole pines along the trail. The deepening shadows had begun to bring a change to the whole landscape. Some high-jutting points of rock looked softer, more rounded-out and close. A few of the lower ridges, on the other hand, gave a feeling that they were moving miles and miles away from the hikers. Even people who were familiar with the country could get confused at a time like this. And tonight there would not even be a moon to help the lost boys see the most obvious landmarks.

Little as Doc liked to walk, he felt the urgency of getting up to the beaver pond while some daylight still remained.

At last they reached the cliff below the beaver pond. There they stopped for another "blow."

"How soon do you figure the Search and Rescue Squad will be here?" Jay asked the sheriff.

"In less than an hour," he answered. "I talked to Ken Schultz, the leader of the Squad, and he said it might take him a while to round up his gang. He always explains to me he can't keep the Squad just sitting together in one room, waiting to get a call to make a rescue."

"I know Ken," Jay said. "He's led college hiking parties up through Payrock a lot of times, and he always stops at the store."

"That's where he's going to stop tonight. I left word with your grandma that he and his men should come straight on from there up to the beaver pond."

This plan made sense to Jay and Doc. They knew that Ashy and the other men from Payrock would go first to Wapiti Camp to report the sheriff's plans. If the kids had returned home in the meantime, Ashy would bring word to the sheriff; if not, all the men would come on up to the beaver pond and help with the search.

Jay didn't put too much faith in the sheriff as a searcher. But he had heard from Ken Schultz a good deal about the work of the Search and Rescue Squad. It was made up of boys and girls from Fremont College, plus a few men from the town of Fremont itself. They were all experienced mountaineers. That meant they didn't just hike up and down long smooth slopes in the Colorado Rockies. They knew scientific ways of climbing sheer cliffs and even of crossing from one cliff-top to another over a deep chasm. They had wonderful light nylon ropes and steel pins called pitons to drive into rocks where safe support was needed. They used this equipment on practice rock-climbs that they were always making just for the fun of it. But it was an important part of their rescue gear, too. In addition, they had light folding stretchers—even one that they could push along on a wheel. They had walkie-talkies they used so that groups could keep in touch with each other, and powerful search-lights which they wore on their hats, so their hands would be free for climbing at night. There was no telling where a rescue job might lead them in the high mountains, so they carried along ice axes to cut footholds in snowbanks and glaciers.

Jay was excited by the fact that he would see the Squad at work. In the last few years, they had performed some almost miraculous life-saving feats. The Squad members did their work because they loved mountain climbing and because they didn't want other people to have accidents.

"A few minutes' search now will be worth hours after daylight has gone," the sheriff said. "Let's get up there and see if we can see any sign that the kids have been around."

Once over the fence, they began to look carefully along the marshy edge of the pond for footprints.

"Even if they came here, you won't find tracks," Doc warned them. "The ground's just like sponge rubber. It springs right back up after you've stepped on it. Look."

He pointed behind them, and their own footsteps in the peatlike soil of the canyon bottom were already disappearing.

"He's right," the sheriff had to admit. "Let's look on higher, dryer ground. We better cross over to the south side, too. That's the side the kids would have come on if they cut across the hill from their camp."

Carefully they picked their way across the crazily heaped-up logs and brush that formed the beaver dam. Then, as if by common agreement, Doc moved into the lead. He had trailed many an animal in the woods, just for the fun of it. Doc began the search on the rising land between the pond and the clifflike wall of the canyon.

Almost before he had started looking, he called back, "They've been here, all right. At least, somebody that's a real greenhorn has been here, messing up the landscape." There at Doc's feet lay scattered orange peels that certainly weren't more than a few hours old. Any experienced hiker knew enough to bury his garbage, no matter if it was only an orange peel.

"I wonder if the kids could swim," Jay said, thoughtfully looking out over the dark water of the pond.

"We won't look in the water till the last thing," the sheriff said. "If they're drowned, they won't get any deader. What I want to do is bring 'em home alive."

Now Doc found a fairly well-marked pair of footprints —just about the right size for an eleven-year-old. "They headed up the canyon," he said. "Now let's see if they came back down."

"If they didn't," Jay said, "they're bound to be around here still, because it's a box canyon. Only experts could get out of here unless they went out the way we came in. What do you say I yell?"

"Go ahead," the sheriff said. "But you're still pretty close to the waterfalls. I don't know as you could hear them if they yelled back."

Jay gave an experimental shout anyway. "Hall-ll-o-o!"

"Hall-ll-o-o! O-o!" came back to him. For a moment he had forgotten what an echo there would be between the two gaunt walls on either side of the canyon. But he called again and then a third time, "Halloo! Hall-oo!"

Then he heard something he thought wasn't quite an echo. He listened and waited. The sound came again. It wasn't an echo of the baritone sound of his own newly changed voice. He felt sure it was a child's cry.

"Did you hear that?" he whispered.

"Yell again," the sheriff said in a low voice. "Just once and then keep quiet. I would have got those kids' names if you hadn't led me up here first, instead of to the camp. It's always better if you can yell a name. That way the person who is lost knows you're looking for him, not just practicing a yodel."

Again the faint childish voice came down to them. It came *down*—the three of them seemed to realize that fact at the same time. They looked upward in the growing dusk along the rock-walled side of the canyon.

"It must be those kids," Jay said. "They're above us, but they seem to be farther up the canyon, too. You know what I bet? I bet they decided they could take a short cut

home by climbing the side of the canyon and cutting back over the ridge to the place where their camp is. Crazy little Texas squirts!"

"What's this about Texas?" the sheriff said. "Most of the lost kids I haul out of the hills were born right here in Colorado. Besides," he added, with a sudden exaggerated drawl, "didn't you-all know I was a Lone Star State boy myself?"

For once Jay had no heart for the crack he always made when someone said he was from Texas—"Well, that's a good place to be *from*." Instead he muttered, "I was just kidding."

A little farther up the canyon, the sheriff signaled for a stop and Jay yelled again. This time the answering voice was closer—in fact, there seemed to be two high-pitched calls for help. But still nothing could be seen.

"You know," the sheriff said, "this is one canyon I've never been up before. What's it like ahead of us?"

"There's another hanging valley, smaller than this one," Jay said. "That's probably where they went."

Jay himself had only seen this particular hanging valley from the ridge above it, but he had always remembered what the geology teacher in the hiking party had told him. An ancient glacier had scoured the canyon out of the very backbone of the Rockies. Grinding its way downward in ages past, the glacier had scooped a U-shaped bed for itself to flow in. At different points in its course, the river of ice had to run over beds of rocks that were harder than others. When it met one of these barriers, the glacier coasted over the hard rock, then dug with renewed ferocity at the softer rock lying just beyond. The result resembled a series of giant steps in the bottom of the canyon. Each of the steps was called a hanging valley.

Soon the boys and the sheriff came to another small waterfall, only half as high as the one below. They scrambled up a heap of broken rock at the side of the falls and were soon on top. It was no use to shout from here with the falls roaring so close to their ears.

"It's a wonder that voices carry back and forth with all this waterfall noise in the canyon," said Jay.

"Yeah, but I've noticed time and again that once you get far enough away from a stream, the water just seems to hum, but voices will carry and echo a long way," Doc said.

The sheriff had something else on his mind. He had turned and faced down the canyon. "Boys," he said, "we'd better stop and build a fire right here on the top of this ledge. Then Ashy and the Payrock fellows and Ken Schultz and his men will see it and know that something's doing up here. It won't hurt the kids either to see that we intend to stay till they're safe—if they got that much sense."

Jay and Doc hurried to gather wood, but they kept glancing down the canyon to see if they could catch sight of the other rescuers. Although the dusk was growing thicker around them, they could still see a golden band of sunlight across the plains far, far down below them and to the east. The last intense rays of the sun seemed to carry their eyes as far as Kansas. But up here, close under the towering Continental Divide, the sheriff had already pulled his flashlight out, ready for use.

While the sheriff kindled a fire not far from the noisy little waterfall, Jay and Doc dragged in some of the aspen that beavers had cut the previous year and left lying on the ground. The flames began to mount, and Jay said to the sheriff, "Bert, hadn't we better go on now and shout some more and have a look while there's still a little light?"

"You boys go ahead, but don't go beyond the end of

this beaver pond. Wait there until either I or the Rescue
Squad fellows join you. Got flashlights?" he added as the
boys turned away.

"Sure thing," they called back.

CHAPTER 6 ... Marooned on a Ledge

A hundred yards back from the falls, Jay and Doc stopped and listened. They heard nothing. Perhaps the lost twins had yelled so much that their voices were giving out.

Jay let loose with another of his resonant calls and then waited for the echo to die down. Immediately the high duet of boyish voices came back, and now it was much more distinct. "Help! Help!" Jay and Doc could make out the words. Still the sound seemed to come from high above them.

"Those crazy kids!" Jay said, less in anger than in awe, as he looked up the forbidding mass of rock on the south side of the hanging valley. "I bet they're stuck on a ledge some place so they can't get up or down. If they'd only wave something white, we could see them."

"If I was stuck on a ledge," Doc said, "I'd be too scared

to move. I'd hold on with both hands and my teeth, too. I probably couldn't even yell."

Jay made a careful, intense study of the rocks above and ahead. At the upper end of the hanging valley there was a huge sloping mass of tumbled rocks and boulders—a talus slope. Beginners might think that this slope offered a way of climbing up to the ridge and out of the valley. Jay had a hunch that the kids had thought they could take a short cut home by climbing the talus slope. But, at the top of it, he knew, was a rock wall. Its chopped-up face was deceptive. It seemed to offer half a dozen different avenues of ascent to the ridge, but any one of them was too steep and dangerous for inexperienced kids who had no climbing equipment.

"Coming!" Jay shouted. Then he set off almost at a trot toward the talus slope. Doc puffed along behind as best he could and reached the great, bewildering heap of stones a few moments after Jay did.

The kids' voices were nearer and clearer now.

"Coming!" Jay yelled again, encouragingly. He turned on his flashlight and waved it in a wide arc with the beam pointed up toward the cliff. It was dark enough now so that the twins could see it and be reassured.

"Look,"—Jay was thinking out loud—"the quicker somebody reaches those kids the better. They may get excited because they know we're coming and do something silly. No matter what's happened to them, they'll feel better if there's somebody there for them to talk to. You wait here and direct the Rescue Squad. I won't try to bring the kids down. I'll stay with them until somebody shows up. You wave your flashlight at the Rescue Squad if you see their flashlights coming. Then they'll know exactly where you are. I'll wave *my* flashlight down toward you when I reach the kids."

Doc was glad enough not to scramble up the talus slope. "I'll scrounge around for some wood," he said, "and build as big a fire as I can right here. That's better than the flashlight."

"Yeah, that'll help me keep my bearings, too," Jay said. Without another word, he turned and began to climb. The first boulders in the slope were enormous jagged chunks of granite-like rock. They had scarcely weathered at all, and sharp edges and points stuck out in any direction. They offered plenty of handholds, and Jay could climb fairly fast. But he knew what lay ahead. Talus is made up of rocks that have broken off from a cliff. The biggest rocks roll the farthest; the small ones pile up behind. Often, right up against the cliff itself, the talus is made of very small stones which are loose and give no solid footing.

The scramble was a tough one, and Jay went as fast as he dared. Soon his lungs were heaving and the heavy throb of his hard-working heart pounded in his ears. His own body made such a racket that he had to stop and rest before he could hear a cry from the twins. Then the kids' voices came to him, much closer. "Here we are!"

Jay waved his flashlight in the direction of the call. Still he couldn't see anybody. It was now almost dark in the canyon. The twins obviously had no flashlight themselves, probably not even any matches.

The going was very tricky from here on. The rocks underfoot were small and slithered out from under Jay as he climbed. The higher he got, the more like quicksand the slope became. He had to be careful not to start a small avalanche of rock coming down upon him. Time and again he had a frustrating feeling of taking step after step in the same spot. Pebbles and coarse gravel slipped out from under the heavy soles of his boots. Then more pebbles slid down to fill in the gaps his feet had made.

Sometimes he was ankle-deep in the loose stuff that seemed almost alive and fighting against him.

At last Jay saw a place where he could go off to the side of the slope and continue on up a ridge of ragged but solid rock. He had learned on hikes before that the longest way round was often the shortest way home. Carefully heaving himself up from one knife-sharp handhold to another, he reached a point where he could brace his back comfortably and shine the light upward.

"Here! Here! Here!" the voices shouted excitedly.

The long beam played in and out among the chimneys and projections of raw rock. Suddenly the light picked out two white spots.

"The little dopes!" Jay muttered to himself. "Got nothing but T-shirts on." He himself was sweating from his climb, but the night air had grown very cold.

"I see you! You all right?" Jay called. Suddenly he realized that the two white T-shirts seemed to be flattened motionless against a sheer face of rock.

"Hurry up!" was the only answer he got. The voice sounded desperate.

Jay kept on solid footing till he reached a point level with the top of the talus slope. Now the solid rock of the cliff was right ahead of him. Keeping his face toward it and clawing at it for support, he sidled quickly along with his feet uncertainly treading the very upper edge of the treacherous heap of loose rock. Soon he had reached a deep cleft or chute in the rock wall. This must have been the place the twins had thought would be an easy route to follow toward the ridge. It was now pitch black in the chute. The bottom of it was made of solid rock that formed a steep upward path. At the end of this, a sudden abrupt wall rose in front. Swinging out over the face of the cliff ran a ledge. The twins must have tried to walk around the ledge. Jay couldn't see them now, but he climbed out onto the ledge and called.

A desperate, strained moan came back. "Hurry up! Hurry up!"

Then Jay's light caught them. They were only about twenty feet ahead, standing on a ledge about two feet wide, flat and rigid against the cliff wall as if they were trying to stick themselves tight to the rock.

And between their ledge and Jay was no ledge at all—nothing—just empty air!

Jay could see the mortal terror in the faces of the two shivering boys.

"Hi!" Jay said cheerfully. "Take it easy, fellows. You'll be off there before long. You all right? Either of you hurt?"

At first the two boys just shook their red heads and blubbered.

"You all right?" Jay repeated.

Still they said nothing, but just blinked through tear-filled eyes at the brilliant flashlight.

"Say!" Jay exclaimed. "Why don't you sit down and take it easy? You've got room enough there." He played the light slowly along the rock ledge at their feet to show them.

The nearest twin choked out, "We're scared to sit down again. It's too dark. We might fall." He began to sob. "Hurry up!"

"Sure, sure," Jay said soothingly. "A whole bunch of men are coming to get you down. They've got ropes and blankets to keep you warm. Everything's going to be all right. Don't you worry."

The redheads began to relax a little, and in the light that Jay kept aimed at the ledge, they eased themselves down and huddled with their backs to the cliff, knees drawn up. Jay could see that they were both shivering

with cold and fear as they pressed against the rock wall.

"Okay, kids, you're safe now," Jay said gently. Below he could see flashlights. The rescue party was already halfway between the sheriff's fire and Doc's. "I can see a whole gang of lights coming. Everything's going to be hunky-dory."

The twins seemed calmed down enough now so that Jay could ask a question that was uppermost in his mind. "Tell me, how did you two fellows get over there, any-way?"

It was obviously the wrong question. Both boys got so choked up with sobs that they couldn't make an answer. Jay searched for something to say that would calm them. He reached into his pocket and pulled out the hard, thick bittersweet chocolate bar he always carried with him on hikes.

"I bet you guys are hungry," he said. "I'm going to toss you over a big bar of chocolate. Don't try to catch it. I'll land it right beside you."

To Jay's amazement, one of the twins wailed with heart-felt anguish, "Chocolate!"

"We're allergic," the other one howled. "Chocolate always makes us wheeze!"

Any other time Jay might have laughed. But now he felt more helpless and miserable himself than he had ever felt on a baby-sitting job.

"Those fellows down below are bringing sandwiches and stuff," he finally thought of saying. He hoped it was true. "What kind do you like best?"

"I want peanut butter and jelly," one twin answered with a little interest, almost calmly.

"Me, too," said the other.

"Okay, it's peanut butter and jelly," Jay said. "Want some hot cocoa—oops—that's got chocolate in it. How about hot soup?"

"Oh, boy!"

"Good!"

"Soup it is, then," Jay said, and he kept up the chatter while he shifted around to get a comfortable seat for himself. He couldn't see a thing he could do to help get the twins off the ledge. Still, if he could find out how they got there in the first place, maybe that would be the key to bringing them down.

Calls came from the party below now. Before answering them, Jay said to the twins, "I'm going to holler, so don't be surprised."

Then, "Okay! Okay!" he shouted out.

From then on at intervals he aimed his flashlight downward and waved it to give the approaching rescue party
its bearings. The redheads seemed calmer, and he decided
to try once more to get their story.

Piecing together what they said, he found what had
happened. That morning the twins' counselor had sprained
his ankle. This meant that the kids would have to spend
the day with a group of younger boys. The idea bored
them, and today seemed a fine opportunity to slip away
unnoticed for a look at the black beavers Jay had talked
about the day he had rounded up the cattle in their camp.
They found the beaver valley without much trouble and
explored all around the lower dam. Then they climbed
into the upper hanging valley to explore some more. Suddenly they realized it was getting late in the afternoon.
They thought that the talus slope offered a short cut home,
and up they went. They had done just exactly as Jay had
figured they would.

When the twins had come to the spot where Jay was
sitting now, the ledge ahead seemed to be a path that
led around a corner and up. They followed along it, holding each other's hands. But they had only gone a little way

when suddenly their weight and the motion of their steps loosened a big section of the ledge that had obviously been just ready to fall. The first twin was able to pull the second one to safety, just as the rock was dropping out from underfoot. In horror they had watched the huge slab of gray rock bound down the talus slope and smash into smaller boulders at the bottom. Then they discovered that the ledge was not a path at all. It tapered off around the corner into nothing. Below them was a sheer fifty-foot drop. There was no way to get ahead or back. They were stuck.

As nearly as Jay could figure out, the kids had been sitting there, calling for help, for three or four hours—maybe even more.

Jay was a good deal more worried now than he dared let the little boys see. Even in daylight it would be no simple thing to rig ropes so that the twins could be lowered from their perch to safety. And now it was dark—pitch dark. Besides, the ledge on which the kids were sitting might easily have been cracked by winter frosts in the past, so that it would break if the weight of rescuers were added to it.

As the search party came closer, Jay began to call directions to the men who had reached the foot of the chute. Suddenly, when his back was turned to the twins, Jay heard a crash of falling rock.

Was the ledge that held the twins giving way?

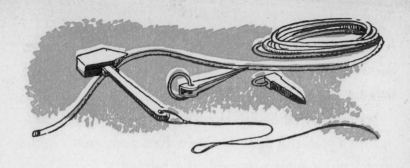

## CHAPTER 7 ... Skill and Nerve

Jay spun around and beamed his light toward the twins. The ledge was still there, and so were the redheads, but one of them was standing up, looking terribly frightened. From below came shouts of alarm.

"What happened, kid?" Jay asked.

"I—I got up, so I could see better," the small boy stuttered out. "I guess I knocked a loose rock over the side."

Jay's impulse was to give the youngster a good bawling out, but he stopped himself short. As calmly as he could, he said, "There'll be plenty of time to see. You just take it slow and sit down again. Make sure you don't scrape anything off the edge this time. There are men down below. You don't want to conk anybody with a rock."

In a moment Jay heard a voice calling to him, "I'm

coming to look things over. Keep your flashlight aimed the other way so it won't get in my eyes." It was Ken Schultz, the leader of the Search and Rescue Squad.

Behind Jay, the cliff face stood in sudden silhouette against a powerful light. He knew Ken was coming up the chute, picking his way with the help of a search lamp attached to his safety helmet.

Presently Ken came around the shoulder of rock and stood out on the ledge beside Jay. He took in the whole picture in an instant. "Hello, young fellows," he said cheerfully to the twins. "Nothing to worry about. We'll have you off there in no time."

Then Jay told Ken quietly about the intervening piece of ledge that had broken off. Ken played his light up and down the empty place.

"It looks to me like a miracle that chunk of rock didn't fall a long time ago," Ken said to Jay. "You can see by the water streaks that there was an old crack behind it. However, the part of the ledge the kids are on now looks perfectly solid," he added. Then he turned and said, "Hold up, you fellows in the chute. There's not room for any more out here. I'll be with you in a minute."

Jay could hear the word being passed down the chute.

"There are seven Squad members here," Ken said, "plus some men from Payrock. This'll be a cinch."

Jay couldn't imagine how getting the twins down would be a cinch.

"By the way," Ken went on, "you did a nice job of locating these kids so quickly. You better come back into the chute now, so you can tell everybody what you know about the setup. Then we can survey the problem and lay out our plans."

Ken took off the thick glasses he wore and wiped them in the light of his search lamp. In the dark, Jay could scarcely see his square-built professorish companion on the ledge, but one thing he knew without looking. Ken's round, very fair face would be pink with the exertion of the climb and probably peeling from sunburn. It almost always was.

"Boys," Ken called to the twins, "we're going back around this corner to get some things ready. You just take it easy and don't worry."

"Give us our peanut butter and jelly sandwiches," one twin called back.

Immediately Jay said, "The sandwiches are down below. You'll get them when you're off that ledge."

"What's this?" Ken asked under his breath.

"The only way I could get them calmed down at first was to promise them peanut butter and jelly," Jay whispered. "I tell you, they're wild men. They'll never thank you for rescuing them, either, unless somebody has peanut butter in his pocket. And don't offer 'em chocolate. They're allergic," he added.

Ken, who was usually solemn, chuckled. "A rescuer's life is not a happy one. Let's get going."

The chute was brilliantly lit by the search lamps that the seven Rescue Squad members wore on their hats. Jay grinned to himself when he saw that two of them were college girls. Let *them* take over the job of solving the sandwich problem.

Ken straddled a little outcropping of rock and acted as chairman of the planning meeting. Jay told what he knew of the terrain. After some discussion, the party divided. Two boys went down and across the top of the talus slope to see if there was an approach to the twins from the other end of their ledge. Two others unslung their packs, got out small hammers, long coils of shiny yellow nylon rope, and the steel spikes with rings in the end which were called pitons. These two rescuers were going to climb up the sheer face at the upper end of the chute to see if they could approach the twins from above.

The remaining man in the party had a very large and cumbersome-looking load on his pack board. Jay could see that the load must be light by the way he easily shifted it off his shoulders and onto a flat spot in the rock.

Ken noticed that Jay was interested. "That's a collapsible stretcher," he explained. "We always have it along just in case there's been an accident."

One of the girls was carrying a strange-looking box slung from a strap over her shoulder. Jay saw that she was studying her wrist watch attentively. In a moment she lifted a telephone receiver out of the box and began to talk into it.

"Walkie-talkie," Ken explained. "We left the other half of it with a Squad member down by the sheriff's fire at the beaver pond. Every half-hour we check in and make reports."

All this was interesting, but it seemed to Jay that the Squad was taking things awfully slow.

"Don't you think you ought to hurry? I'm worried about those kids," he said to Ken. "No fooling, they haven't got enough sense between the two of them to please a pumpkin. They might do almost anything."

"There are some things you can't do in a hurry," Ken said. "We have to know exactly what the lay of the land is."

Reluctantly Jay said, "I suppose I better go back and talk to the kids and keep them calmed down."

By now hammers were ringing in the chute where the two climbers found cracks into which they could drive the pitons. Jay watched for a moment as they rigged ropes through the holes in the pitons and then, holding themselves by their ropes, seemed to walk by slow stages up the face of the cliff.

After what seemed an endless conversation with the twins, Jay heard Ken calling him back into the chute. All four climbers had returned. The two who had gone along the talus slope reported there was no easy way up to the ledge from the other side. The two who had climbed the cliff at the back of the chute reported a broad ledge about twenty feet above the one on which the twins were stranded.

All hands agreed that there was only one thing to do. Operating from the upper ledge, two Squad members would rope themselves down to the twins. There they would hitch each boy into a kind of chair made of rope. Then they would lower them one at a time to the talus slope below.

Jay listened quietly to the plan, then he blurted out, "Excuse me, Ken, but I don't think you know what kind of kids we have on our hands. They're so scared I don't think they'd go over the side. They might get hysterical and put up a fight." He paused, then asked, "Do you suppose you could rig up some way to lower them in that folding litter?"

Ken hesitated, and Jay went on, "I could tell them it's just like going down in an elevator. I could make them think it's safe—if it is," he added, half doubtfully.

"It would be safe enough if we lashed them in," Ken said.

"We've practiced that kind of rescue a lot of times," one of the girls said. "Maybe we could even bring them both down in the litter at the same time. I'm sure they'd feel better about that."

"I think you've hit it," Ken said. "If everybody agrees, this will be a job of evacuation by litter."

Jay heaved a sigh of relief. He felt better about another thing, too. The Squad really began to go into action now.

Ken took off up the rope-and-piton route to the ledge above, followed by two other husky college boys, one of them carrying the litter on his back.

One of the girls saw that Jay's flashlight was getting quite weak. She took off her helmet and quickly unstrapped the belt that held the battery. "Here," she said to Jay, "you'll want this while you're out there talking to the twins. This light is better than yours and it will help the fellows while they're getting the poor little things into that litter."

Jay appreciated her kindness both for his own sake and the twins', but he figured she would feel a little less motherly when she met the redheads in person. Grimly he thought to himself, she had better scare up that sandwich or a reasonable facsimile thereof.

With his new light, Jay went back and talked to the twins. He told them that Ken was going to bring a special elevator to take them down. Boy, would they have something to tell the other kids back at camp! Soon the attention of the two restless redheads was drawn to a regular circus stunt in the light of the rescuers' search lamps.

From above the twins, Ken gave careful instructions. "Don't budge from where you're sitting. I'm coming

right down the face of this rock. When I get to your ledge, don't move either. Stay absolutely quiet until I tell you what to do."

Jay took up where Ken left off. "That man's name is Ken. He's the boss. Everything he's going to do is safe. He knows just what he's doing. He won't fall."

"Here goes!" Ken called. Facing the cliff, he began to walk quickly down, like a fly!

Jay couldn't help holding his breath every time he saw this trick done. It was called rappelling. First Ken ran his rope through metal rings he had fastened solidly to pitons driven in the rock at the top of the cliff. Then he took the two thicknesses of nylon rope and passed them between his legs. The rope came up around his right hip, across his chest, over his left shoulder and across his back down to his right side. His left hand held the rope out in front of him. Then, leaning way out against the rope that crossed his back, he walked down the cliff, letting the rope slide gradually through his two hands and around his body. All this friction kept him secure. In no time at all he was standing beside the twins on the ledge.

A minute later, another Squad member rappelled down, using a second nylon rope. Ken and his companion gave their windbreakers to the half-frozen twins. Then the rescuers tied their ropes around their own bodies for safety.

Now they began to drive more pitons into small cracks of rock about shoulder height above the ledge.

"Ready for the ropes," Ken called to a third man standing at the top of the cliff above him.

Two nylon ropes came down. Ken ran the ropes through the rings in the pitons and dropped one end of each rope to the Rescue Squad men standing on the talus slope below.

"Lower away!" Ken called to the man above him.

"Here comes your elevator, kids," Jay announced to the twins. There, suspended from a small nylon cord, came the featherweight aluminum litter.

It had been assembled and looked like a long, narrow basket big enough to hold a full-grown man. When it reached the ledge, Ken worked at the ropes expertly. Soon he had it fixed so that the litter could be lowered to the talus slope, using the rings in the pitons for pulleys.

All this time the twins had kept amazingly quiet. Their eyes had been fixed with complete fascination on the elevator that was being rigged up for them to ride in. They could hardly contain themselves now, as they watched Ken methodically testing every piton and knot to make sure it was all secure.

Then Ken announced, "Well, I guess it's about ready now." He stood up and leaned inward for a moment's rest with his head on his arms against the rock face. The arch that his body made over the narrow ledge seemed a perfect doorway to the twin nearest him. Quick as a rabbit, the redhead scrambled toward the litter, between Ken's knees and the wall.

Startled, Ken took an involuntary step backward—into empty space.

CHAPTER 8 . . . Danger in the Night

Paralyzed with horror and fear, Jay saw Ken topple away from the ledge. An image of Ken's body crushed on the rocks below flashed across his mind. Jay's insides seethed into a tight knot. The next instant a powerful tug on Ken's body stopped it in midair. There he stayed, dangling over the outer rim of the ledge. His safety rope had caught him.

Heaving up with his strong arms, Ken swung himself back onto the ledge. There he lay flat and panted from the sudden fear that had filled him.

The first sound was a jumble of cries from rescuers who stood on the talus slope below. Then the other Squad member on the ledge found his voice. With incredible calm he said to the twin, "Don't you move one inch!" Then, "Are you okay, Ken?"

"Yeah. Just let me rest a minute," Ken answered.

Presently he pulled himself upright, standing close to the rock wall, while strength returned to his shaking knees. He took one enormously deep breath like a sigh, and Jay saw by his stance that he was ready to return to business. With silent firmness more commanding than words, he held the litter steady and motioned for the reckless twin to crawl carefully over into it.

"Lie down, with feet toward the middle," Ken ordered, in a hard steady voice.

Stiffly, as if all his joints had frozen, the boy followed instructions.

"Now, *stay* there. Don't sit up," Ken commanded.

Immediately, as if he doubted the kid's ability to obey instructions, the other Squad member on the ledge wove rope back and forth over the top of the litter so that its small passenger was securely lashed in. Very soon the other twin was lying in position at the other end of the litter. He, too, was secured with rope lashing.

Almost at the same moment the two of them began to wail, "I'm scared! Let me out of here! I'm scared!"

This part of the job done, Ken took off his glasses and polished them. It was a habit he had when he was resting or thinking. Turning to Jay, he called, "Jay, were you ever right! They're mavericks, but we have them hog-tied and they can't cause any trouble for a minute or two."

Then over the side of the ledge, Ken shouted to the members of the Squad below, "All set? Hoist when I give the signal."

At his call, the litter basket rose off the ledge amid terrified shrieks from within it. "Out on the guy ropes!" Ken shouted. Two rescuers below had ropes with which they pulled the litter out away from the cliff so it wouldn't bump against projecting rocks. "All clear. Lower away slow and easy," Ken directed.

Now, hanging out over space, the wailing basketload of redheads moved slowly down the face of the cliff.

As the basket disappeared, Jay stretched himself in relief. Then he turned and scrambled down the chute. When he reached the talus slope, the twins were standing in the glare of a circle of search lamps, wrapped to their ears in blankets—and munching sandwiches.

"Peanut butter and jelly?" Jay asked the walkie-talkie girl with a malicious grin.

"They certainly are just that," said a voice from behind her. It was Doc.

"Where did you blow in from?" Jay asked. He had been

too absorbed in the rescue even to think about Doc.

"Oh, I've turned mountain guide," Doc answered. "I covered more ground tonight than you did, lazybones."

"Who are you kidding!" Jay snorted. "You left your horse at home."

"Ask anybody," Doc said. "It was me that brought those peanut butter and jelly sandwiches."

"How come?" Jay asked incredulously.

"No fooling. When the Rescue Squad got to my fire at the foot of the talus slope, they told me to go on back down and help the sheriff. They said his fire was going to be their base camp and maybe I could be useful there. By the time I got there, this dame with the walkie-talkie had given Bert quite a spiel. She said these kids needed special food—nothing but peanut butter and jelly. It wasn't enough for them to be lost. They had to have allergies, too. Bert asked me and Ashy to hike on down with him to his car. He had to use his radio to let his office know that the kids were safe. The telephone up this way was working again so Bert's office phoned the kids' camp. Just for the heck of it, I got Bert to put in an order for peanut butter and jelly. Then I waited for a car to come from Wapiti. Bert asked me to guide the counselors all the way up here. To tell you the truth, Bert asked Ashy first, but the old boy was cranky as all get out. He said he wasn't going to lose any more sleep—for anybody. So I had to come, and boy, am I tired!"

A minute later, the two boys fell in at the tail end of the march downhill which Ken had organized. As they shuffled wearily along, Jay answered Doc's questions about the rescue. Then for a long time the whole party walked in silence. The twins were nearly asleep on their feet as Squad members helped them along.

When they reached the edge of the beaver pond, Ken signaled for a rest.

"That reminds me," Doc said to Jay, "I saw something interesting here on my way down the first time. I gave myself orders to stop and have a 'blow'—not your stingy kind, but a real good one. I sat down and turned off my flashlight to save it, and pretty soon I heard a beaver waddling through the brush. It seemed like a good time to find out if he'd turned from black to brown. He was sure surprised when I shot my light at him. I got a good look, and that metal clip in his ear showed up as plain as anything. He was a black one, all right."

"I guess the jinx hasn't got 'em yet, anyway," said Jay.

"Let's *go!*" Ken called out.

"He's almost as bad as you are," Doc groaned and began to pull himself to his feet.

"There's hot soup right ahead at base camp," the walkie-talkie girl announced cheerily to the twins who were the last ones to stand up.

Then, just as the party resumed its slow shuffle homeward, everyone froze in his tracks. From high above them came a deep, explosive rumble. The canyon filled with echoes, and the noise bore down on them. Suddenly it was close—very close. Then it ended in a series of loud reports like gunshots in the aspen grove they had just passed through. The canyon was silent again, except for the rattle of small loose stones.

The silence lasted only an instant. The twins set up a terrified wailing.

"What happened? What was that?" a Wapiti counselor bellowed, nearly as frightened as the twins.

Jay was certain he knew. Some enormous boulder had fallen from the high ridge above. It must have been a big one—when it crashed into the aspens it snapped them off and made them crack like gunfire.

"Lucky we weren't back in those trees just now," Jay

said. But he was puzzled, and Doc was, too. At this time of year, it was very unusual for big boulders to break loose from cliffs. The violent shifts between freezing and thaw-ing in early spring often caused cracks in rocks, and great slabs would drop away. Now it was August, the warmest month in the mountains, and although it was chilly tonight it wasn't freezing.

Today there had been not one but two falls of rock in this same canyon. It just didn't make sense.

## CHAPTER 9 ... The Man with the Box

For the next few days, Jay and Doc spent a lot of time riding in the canyon of the North Fork of Payrock Creek. They were having a kind of running argument with the Circle M cattle. Even though it was still August, thin sheets of ice appeared morning after morning on quiet pools of water high up on the range. The cattle didn't like the cold, and they moved stubbornly down toward warmer land, away from the ridges above timberline. And just as stubbornly, Doc and Jay tried to keep them on high ground where the grass was still good.

Today was warmer. The critters were staying put in high country, and the two boys had had a leisurely time of it under the clear, brilliant sun. But now the clouds began to pile up for the regular afternoon shower. At the first few drops the boys made for a stand of Engelmann spruce, dismounted, and squatted under the natural umbrella formed by the thick, sloping branches of one of the trees.

"Riding old Buck sure beats slogging along on foot the way we did the other night," Doc said. "The muscles on top of my legs are still sore from all that climbing I did."

"Here we go again," Jay said with a grin. "But you got to admit you had a good time."

Doc nodded silently. After a pause Jay went on, "You know, I can't help thinking about all the things those fellows in the Rescue Squad could do. The way they worked with their gear was sure neat." Jay paused again and scratched meaningless doodles in the thick layer of gray-brown needles on which he sat. "You know, I'd give my right arm if they'd let me be a member of the Squad. But I know what they'd say. They're all college kids at least, and they'd say I was too young."

"You'd be a heck of a rescuer without a right arm," Doc joshed him. "But why don't you ask them? No harm to ask."

"No. I bet it's like those swanky college frats. You have to wait for *them* to ask you."

"Didn't you say they give classes to teach rock climbing and rescue work?" Doc asked. "I bet they wouldn't try to keep you out of that. It's not a regular college class, because the Squad runs it by itself."

"I guess there's no harm in asking Ken the next time I see him," Jay said.

The shower was over now, and the boys crawled out from under the tree. Jay stood up. His eyes swept the giant rock walls that rimmed the North Fork canyon. Nothing in the world seemed so important to him right then as having the gear and the know-how with which to master those challenging heights. Most of the canyon was once again filled with afternoon sunlight. It was time to turn the horses downstream and amble on home to Payrock.

Just above the junction of the North Fork with Payrock Creek, Doc reined Buck in. "Hi!" he called to someone ahead. When Jay pulled up beside him, he saw Ashy with his rucksack on his back. The old man had apparently come down from somewhere above them and had just reached the trail.

"Hi!" said Jay.

"I was hoping to get here in time to catch you," Ashy said brusquely. He almost never greeted people. "I've got something for you to show your dad," he announced, looking at Doc. He swung the rucksack off his back, and as he dropped it to the ground a clank of iron on iron told the boys that Ashy had been spending his time as usual—picking up old spikes and bolts and such to sell as scrap metal. Probably he had been at the mine dump not far above them in the timber. He rummaged in the rucksack and pulled something out.

"Here," Ashy said, handing Doc two objects that looked like curled-up scraps of cowhide.

"Ears!" Doc exclaimed. "This one came from a Circle M critter and the other's a Bar Forty." Doc recognized them because of the earmarks that had been cut out of them. His father's distinctive mark was a notch in the underside of the ear, called an "underslope." And the Bar Forty ranch owned the only cattle on this part of the range that had a simple split cut in the end of each ear. Some of these animals grazed with the Circle M cattle and weren't separated until roundup time.

"Where in the world did you get these?" Doc asked with sudden serious concern. The ears had been cut off cleanly with a knife. Were there rustlers butchering cattle up here and leaving telltale ears behind? Rustlers never had worked over this range, but maybe that was a good reason why they would want to start operations now.

"I cut 'em off two dead steers under a cliff below the lowest beaver pond on the Middle Fork," Ashy answered. "Looked to me like something stampeded them over the cliff. One steer might wander over the edge by accident—but not two in the same place. I took the ears so your dad and the Bar Forty fellow would know about it. Looks to me like you'd be smart to get your cattle off that part of the range."

"I guess you're right," Doc said. "There's been nothing but trouble over there all summer. Thanks a lot, Ashy. Are the hides worth saving?"

"I dunno," Ashy answered. "They're kind of tore up. A bear had already found 'em before I got there. And you know how a bear leaves a hide. He just peels it off in strips."

This was the third time cattle had been spooked in the area this month, Jay thought. Something was wrong, no doubt about it.

"Ashy, do you think somebody would be stampeding our stock on purpose?" Doc asked. "Have you seen anybody that doesn't belong around here?"

"Summer people are thick as mosquitoes," Ashy grumbled. "But I only seen one guy that seemed to act funny. He's all over this country, and he always keeps to himself. The way you'll know him is he travels around with a funny kind of box hanging at his side. Three or four times I've tried to catch up with him so I could take a good look, but when I got there he was always some place else. Between you and me, he acts plumb crazy."

"You'd have to be crazy to go around spooking cattle for no good reason," Doc said. "Well, I'll tell my dad. Thanks again."

"I wouldn't be surprised," Ashy went on, "if that crazy guy was poisoning the mountain sheep, too."

"Say, you reminded me of something I almost forgot to tell you," Jay said. "Van came by the store last night. He said the laboratory people found out what killed the sheep. It was lung-worm disease, whatever that is."

"Humph!" said Ashy. "Never heard of it and I've lived here all my life. It's probably some newfangled germ, and I wouldn't wonder if the crazy guy is spreading that around, too."

He picked up his rucksack, and without even saying "So long," he headed across the creek, stepping from boulder to boulder, along a short cut toward his cabin high up on the South Fork.

For a while the boys rode down the trail in silence. Then Jay said, "I think we better move those critters, starting tomorrow."

"It looks that way. I'll ask Dad," Doc answered. "Say! Look ahead. There's a guy with something that looks like a box!"

Jay touched Maude and caught up with Doc who was riding ahead. Through the willows near the stream he saw the figure of a man, and there *was* something hanging at his side. Jay laughed, "That's a fishing basket. You're so hopped up about your steers you're seeing things."

As the trail brought them close to where the man was standing, Jay called out, "How are they biting?"

"Don't know," the man answered. "I just got here. But if they behave the way they have been all week, I won't get a nibble. There are plenty of trout here, but they seem determined to spoil my vacation. Somebody must have put a spell on them."

Jay and Doc looked at each other. "You mean they're jinxed, too?" said Doc. "Just about everything in Payrock Canyon seems to be jinxed!"

There was something in the fervent way he said it that made the man look up from the trout fly he was attaching to his line. "Has there been some trouble around here?" he asked.

"You said it!" Doc answered.

"Didn't you hear about the kids getting lost just over that ridge?" Jay asked.

"No—I haven't seen a paper," the man answered. "I'm on vacation."

"The kids aren't all," Doc put in. "Our cattle have been stampeded a lot of times. Look at this if you don't believe me." He pulled the two ears out of the pocket of his flannel shirt.

The fisherman put down his pole and came closer. He was plainly interested. "Tell me about it," he said.

The boys gave him their whole long tale of woes— about the stampede through the camp and how mad the Wapiti people were, about Van's beaver that turned from black to brown, about the mountain sheep that were dying, the aspens that had lost their green color, about the rock that had fallen almost on top of the rescue party. They wound up with Ashy's theory that the mysterious man with the box was behind some of the trouble.

The more they talked, the more the fisherman led them on with interested questions. Finally he said, "Well, thanks a lot for the information, boys. All this will make a swell story."

Curiously Jay asked, "What do you mean story? It's true."

The man laughed. "I should have explained. I'm a writer, and I want to make a story out of all this interesting stuff you've told me. No objections, I hope."

"No," said Jay, "it sure is interesting and mysterious. I expect that you could make the whole thing into a good story."

"We better mosey on, Jay," said Doc.

"I hope your luck changes, mister," Jay told the fisherman. "It's about the time of day when they should bite."

Soon the boys reached the road that led in great S-turns down toward the town of Payrock. Before Jay let Maude have her head for a gallop in the direction of home and a pan of oats, he called over his shoulder to Doc, "Say, we should have asked that fellow. I wonder what kind of story he's going to write."

Then, before Doc could answer, Jay pulled Maude to a sudden stop. "Look!" he almost whispered, pointing to something he had seen as he turned his head.

There, on an exposed shoulder of the mountainside, sharply outlined in the late afternoon sun, stood a man. A box hung at his side.

## CHAPTER 10 ... Jinx of Payrock Canyon

The afternoon rush in Grandma Himrod's store was almost over. People had finished shopping, picked up their mail, and left. Now Van Hollister stood at the phone reporting to his office on his day's work for the Game and Fish Department. The only customer was Jerrold George III, who had come in late with an enormous order. Although the store was quiet, Jay was hurrying. Mr. George had a way of insisting on a lot of service, and fast.

Grandma sat stiffly upright on her stool behind the cash register. With her usual gesture of impatience, she put on her glasses. It always seemed to her an unnecessary weakness that her aging eyes needed spectacles. Her motions indicated that will power—and she had plenty of that— ought to be able to make her eyes focus clearly on even small type. As Jay hurried from one end of the store to the other, getting cans and packages off the shelves, she opened the Denver *Gazette,* which had just come, and began to read.

"Great jumping toads!" Grandma exclaimed suddenly. "Here's a big piece about Payrock! It's labeled 'The Jinx of Payrock Canyon.' What do you make of that?"

Jay dropped a can of tomatoes on the counter.

"Listen to this," Grandma began to read aloud. " 'A mysterious jinx is throwing a devastating blight over life, whether it be plant, animal, or human—' "

Jay waited to hear no more. "Excuse me," he said to Jerrold George III and disappeared through the door at the back of the store. When he came back from telephoning the news to Doc on their private wire, Grandma looked at him accusingly. "It says here, 'My informants, two intelligent young cowboys, thoroughly familiar with the area, gave me my first lead to this intriguing mystery. Later evidence gathered from official sources confirms it.' There's a lot more of this balderdash," Grandma said. "You wouldn't have any idea who the young cowboys were, would you, Jay?"

By now Grandma sounded very angry. Jay couldn't understand it, and he was too amazed to answer.

"You know what this means, don't you?" Grandma went on. "Half those tourists from Denver who usually come up here for the last week of summer will be scared away. They'll go some place else this year. This town will lose plenty of business."

Running footsteps thundered on the wooden platform outside the store, and Doc burst in. "Let me see that story about the jinx! What does it say?" he demanded joyfully.

"More telepathy, I suppose," Mr. George growled in annoyance. "Will you *please* finish my order!"

Jay pushed the last of the cans and packages down the counter. Then, while Grandma added the bill up, he took the paper from her lap and motioned for Doc to come and read it quietly.

"That's sure bad medicine for Payrock," Van said sympathetically. "How did you fellows get mixed up with a newspaper reporter?"

"We didn't know. He just said he was going to write a story. And he didn't even say *that* until we'd talked to him for a long time. We didn't tell him anything but the truth. But then he turned around and made it all sound pretty terrible," Jay answered. "Besides, there really *is* something wrong up here."

"Jay's right," Doc added. "My dad thinks so, too. He and I have been working the cattle over to another part of the range these last two days."

Mr. George waited a few moments by the cash register, obviously expecting Jay to pick up the box of groceries and carry it to his car. But Jay's mind was on other things. Finally, the man impatiently shouldered out through the screen door with the big box in his arms.

Now Jay looked belligerently at Grandma. He didn't tell lies, and he certainly hadn't told any to this newspaperman. Besides, he hadn't known the guy was a writer at first. Jay was braced for a good lecture from Grandma, so he was surprised when she said:

"Well, I don't know as I can blame you boys too much. Many's the time I've said things before strangers that I was sorry for later. Himrods generally say what's on their minds, whether it's the smart thing to do or not."

"Actually," Van said in a quiet voice, "there's more bad luck floating around up here than either you or that reporter know about. Two men from my department came up to look over the mountain sheep and see what should be done about the epidemic of lung-worm disease that's broken out. They found a mighty strange thing, and besides that they came near being killed in a rock slide."

"Has somebody been giving lung disease to the sheep?" Doc asked, thinking immediately of the mysterious man with the box.

"It amounts to that, but it's not so simple," Van answered.

In order to explain, Van had to tell a little about how the Game and Fish Department cared for the scattered bands of mountain sheep in the high Rockies. For one thing, the Department put out blocks of salt for the animals to lick. Salt helped to keep them healthy. Usually the sheep stayed around pretty close to the salt lick, and this place was called their "bedding ground." If they used the same bedding ground year after year, it got very unsanitary. One way to keep the animals moving to new and healthy bedding grounds was to move the salt from place to place.

"What do you mean 'unsanitary'?" Jay asked.

"A sheep gets sick from lung worms and it begins to cough. The stuff it coughs up has little baby worms in it," Van answered. "If it goes on coughing in the same place, for a long time, there are millions of these worms scattered all over the ground."

"I see," Jay said. "Then the worms get into some of the

other sheep and make *them* sick."

"It's a heap more interesting than that," Van said. "These little lung worms crawl into the bodies of snails first. While the worm is in the snail's body, it grows up and turns into something that looks like a tadpole. Now, this tadpole finally crawls out of the snail onto a piece of grass and goes to sleep. Along comes Mr. Bighorn, eats the blade of grass, and before long he's coughing with the lung-worm disease."

Doc was fascinated by this piece of nature lore that he had never heard before. Jay was interested, too. But he was a step ahead of the others. "What is the connection between all this and the strange thing you found out, Van?" he asked.

"I'm coming to that. Some low-down human coyote took the salt from where we put it and lugged it right back near the sheep's old bedding ground. There wasn't any way in the world those sheep could *keep* from getting big doses of lung worm spread all through the flock. No wonder they are dying. I'd sure like to catch whoever did that dirty trick."

"Why do you suppose anybody would want to kill the sheep off?" Doc asked.

"I don't know if anybody did it on purpose, but somebody did it, and the sheep are dying," Van answered.

"It doesn't make sense," said Grandma. "I think you are making a lot out of nothing. It was probably some tenderfoot tourist who thought he was doing the sheep a good turn."

"You know," Jay said, "there's a queer guy hiking all over the mountains around here. We saw him ourselves the other day, and Ashy told us he has seen the man a lot of times. Ashy says he acts queer and carries a funny-looking box everywhere. We saw the box, too."

"Nonsense," said Grandma. "It was a tourist with a camera."

"I thought of that," Jay said. "But the box didn't look like a camera box. And besides, Ashy says the fellow is always trying to duck out of sight."

Grandma's certainty that the mysterious man was a tourist began to waver. "I can't deny that your cattle got stampeded, Doc," she said. "Maybe the same person spooked the cows and monkeyed with the salt."

"And did a whole lot of other things," Jay put in enthusiastically. "Maybe this crazy guy pushed the big rock off the cliff when we were bringing the twins home."

"That reminds me of something else screwy," Van said. "When the two fellows went up there to look at the sheep, they almost didn't get back. They were lugging the salt to where it belonged and all of a sudden a rock slide started. They might have got killed if they hadn't been quick on their feet. And they swore it wasn't a natural slide. They heard something that sounded like a blast of dynamite before the rocks started down the hill at them."

"Dynamite!" both boys exclaimed at once.

"I bet that crazy man is carrying around a detonating box," Jay said.

"He would sure have to be crazy to do that," Grandma said. She had been around mining camps long enough to know that all you needed to explode a stick of dynamite was a fuse, a cap, and a match, unless you planned to blow up the whole side of a mountain.

Everyone was silent then. Jay heard a scratching at the screen door. This was Benzy's signal that he wanted to come in. Through the screen Jay saw that the squat yellow pooch had something in his mouth.

"Oh-h, not again!" he groaned. He opened the door and Benzy wiggled in, his long body vibrating all over with satisfaction. In his mouth was a bundle of magazines or something tied loosely with brown post-office string. Jay grabbed the bundle and groaned again. "He's got somebody's mail."

"Whose?" Grandma demanded.

Jay turned the package over, and there staring at him on a wrapper around one of the publications were the words: *Jerrold George III, Sky High Ranch, Payrock, Colo.*

"Well?" said Grandma.

Just then the string around the bundle came loose. A seed catalogue, a fancy folder advertising ladies' fur coats, and a sporting goods catalogue fell to the floor.

"Well!" Grandma said again.

"At least he didn't swipe any letters or valuable mail," Jay said defensively.

"Well, who does it belong to? You have to take it back," said Grandma impatiently.

"Mr. George. Benzy must have got into his station wagon again," Jay said with every sign of acute misery. The Sky High Ranch was a good ten miles away. It would be just like Grandma to say he must hike over there and back tonight. She was that way about making Jay return things that didn't belong to him, even if it was only a darned old fur coat catalogue.

Grandma just looked at him.

"All right," he said. "Doc, can I ride Maude?"

Van chuckled. "Take it easy. I'll run you over in my truck. I should go and look at a beaver dam near George's place anyway. There's a complaint that beavers have flooded a horse pasture in the bottomland there."

As they rode along, Van talked about beavers. He really liked the amazing little animals, even when they caused trouble by damming up streams in the wrong places. "I may have to clear them out of this place I'm going to. It's getting kind of late in the season to transplant them, but I think I'll try. You kids want to give me a hand?"

## CHAPTER 11 ... Beaver Information

Jay ran toward Van's pickup truck which was parked in front of the Sky High ranch house.

"Whew! That was lucky," he said as he climbed in and sat down beside Doc. "I didn't have to explain anything about Benzy."

"How come?" Doc asked.

"I knocked on the door and it was like a movie. A woman who works there came out in a black dress and a fancy white apron and a silly-looking cap on her head. I just had to tell her here was some mail Mr. George lost, and then I scrammed."

"George has sure fixed this old ranch up," said Van. "Swimming pool and palomino horses and maids."

"He's even got his own plane," Jay added. "He can fix it up to land anywhere, too—on water or snow, even."

Van turned the pickup into the long private road that led to the ranch house. Then, a couple of miles down the highway, he parked near a bridge and told the boys to come along with him up the creek.

Scrub willow made the going slow for a way, as they followed the rocky creek bank. Then, ahead of them, stood a dam three or four feet high across the stream. Logs, branches, and twigs, crisscrossed every which way and plastered with mud, made a solid barrier against the water behind. Above the dam, the canyon bottom widened out into a large, flat, open area. A barbed-wire fence, now partly under water, marked the outline of a pasture which the beaver dam had flooded.

"You can't blame a rancher for getting mad when he loses a good pasture like this," Van said. "We'll sure enough have to clear this place out."

The three of them went back the short distance to the road and from the rear of the pickup they took four objects made with metal frames surrounded by wire mesh. These were live-traps for beavers, Van explained. They were shaped like large suitcases.

"I want to be sure these fellows are caught when I come back in the morning," Van said. "So here's what I'm going to do. I'm going to tear a hole in their dam. That will lower the water level and the beavers will rush over to start making repairs. I'll set the traps all around the hole and I'll put some of this good old bait in them. The beavers will fall for the bait and get caught."

"What do you use for bait?" Jay asked.

"I got my own secret formula," Van answered.

"Aw, go on," said Jay.

"Yes, I have. Every good beaver trapper in the country has his own formula, and not a one of them will tell you what it is. I'll say this much—three of the things I put in it are fish oil, an oil that smells a little bit like licorice, and castor."

"Castor oil!" Jay exclaimed.

"Yeah, but not the kind you're thinking of," Van said with a grin. "This is beaver castor that I use. It comes from a gland under the tail, and it has a musky smell. Believe it or not, they say that musk is used in ladies' perfume. I get the castor glands when I take beavers for the pelts. Then I grind the castors up into a kind of creamy orange stuff. Beavers can smell it a quarter of a mile away. Mixed with my other secret ingredients, it always fetches 'em."

The boys helped Van, heaving and tugging at the

branches and sticks of the beaver dam. They watched fascinated as he set the traps at the edge of the water near the hole in the dam. Each trap was opened and attached firmly to a stake pounded in the earth of the dam. One side of the open trap stuck out above water. Van then put some fresh-cut twigs in the center of the exposed part of the trap. Next he opened a bottle that he took from his pocket.

"Want to smell my bait, boys?" he asked.

"Whew! It stinks!" said Jay.

"Sure does, but the beavers go for it like kids after candy."

Van poured a few drops of the scent on the fresh twigs in each trap. "Now, when the little fellers come and sniff this bait, they'll step on the trigger in the bottom part of the trap, and it'll snap shut. Unless there's an accident, a beaver isn't hurt at all, and he won't drown, either. The top of the trap is up out of the water so he can get air. I bet we'll see some results tomorrow."

"I don't see any beavers now," Jay said.

"Don't you worry. They'll come running pretty soon. They don't want the water level in their pond to drop," Van said.

"Why not?" Jay asked.

"I know that much," Doc put in. "It wouldn't be safe for them. If the water drains away, a coyote or bobcat or mountain lion could chase them clear up to their house. Beavers can't run worth anything, but they can swim away from almost any enemy."

"There's another reason, too," Van said. "Somewhere out there under the water, there's a big pile of aspen and willow branches. That's the beavers' winter food supply for the whole family. The bark keeps a lot fresher under water than it does on dry land, and bark's what they eat."

"Gee, I wish we could stay and watch one get caught," said Doc.

"You can stay if you want to, but I gotta get going," Van answered.

Reluctantly the boys decided to go with him. It was too late to think of walking all the way home to Payrock, and besides, they were hungry.

Next morning, they were back with Van bright and early. Doc was so eager to see the animals that he ran most of the way from the pickup truck to the dam.

"You got three of them," he called excitedly.

The big jaws of the live-traps had closed around two full-grown beavers and one little kit that Van told them was just about four months old.

"We're lucky we got 'em all," Van added. "Sometimes beavers get wise to these traps, and then you have to come back with a different kind."

"How do you know you got them all?" Doc asked.

"I'm not absolutely sure, of course, but the rancher here reported he thought there was only one pair and one kit. They usually have two or three or even four kits in the spring. The other little ones must have got washed downstream when a spring flood tore a hole in the dam."

Van pulled the traps out of the water and laid them on the bank. Then, with a special pair of pliers, he fastened numbered metal tags in the animals' ears while they were held securely between the wire mesh jaws. Next he opened the jaws slightly, and with quick, sure movements he slipped a gunnysack over the first beaver's head.

"Here, you hold this guy while I take the next one," said Van, thrusting the sack at Jay.

Doc held the second big beaver in its sack while Van began to get the kit out of its trap. "Gee, he's a cute little fellow," said Doc. "I bet he'd make a good pet."

"Yeah, I had one once," Van answered. "He followed me around the yard like a dog. But it's kind of a nuisance

getting food for them. And besides, you can't ever tell
what kind of temper they're going to have. Some beavers
have good dispositions and some don't—just like people."

Carrying the three bags they went back to the truck. Van
had brought along a cage for them to ride in, but before
he put them in he said, "Now comes the paper work."
He hung each sack from scales. After weighing it, he
worked the sack around so that the beaver's tail stuck out.
Using a flexible steel tape measure, he measured the length
and breadth of the tail and the size of the feet.

"What are you doing all this for?" Doc wanted to know.

"Taking care of beavers is scientific work," Van answered. "We want to know how fast they grow, how big
they get, how far they can travel if they decide to move from
the place where we put them—a whole slew of things.
We'll learn a lot about these fellows when we catch them
again. That's what the ear tags and measurements are for.
All the dope goes down in records next to the number on
the ear clip. I call it my F.B.I. file."

"Yeah!" said Jay skeptically.

"Sure, F.B.I.—For Beaver Information," said Van with
a grin.

Holding the base of the tail in one hand and grabbing

a hind foot in the other, Van lifted each beaver up and put it into the cage. Soon the family of sleek brown animals was on its way in the truck toward a new stream fifteen miles to the north.

Turning off the main road, Van drove the pickup truck over the remains of a bumpy old logging road. When he could go no farther into the woods, he and the boys hopped out.

"It's not far. We'll carry the whole cage," Van said. Two of them holding it at a time, they took the cage a few hundred yards to an aspen grove that stood at the edge of a clear mountain stream.

"It's a good place for a dam right here," Van said, "—if the beavers only have sense enough to stay. You never know. Sometimes they get ideas of their own. Could be they'll go back home. A fifteen-mile walk across country is nothing for them. Or it could be they'll end up on the other side of this ridge in the North Fork."

Jay looked questioningly up the hillside. It was hard for him to believe that a beaver would climb the steep slope and make its way through the fallen timber. He studied the bald mountain ridge that lay between them and the North Fork of Payrock Creek. "Do you mean—" he began, and then his question stopped in midair.

There, in a spot on the lower slope that was left exposed by an old forest fire, where weathered gray tree trunks leaned against an outcropping of rock, stood the man with the box!

## CHAPTER 12 ... Trailing in the Tundra

Jay poked Doc and said almost in a whisper, "There he is again—up there." He pointed.

"The crazy guy!" Doc exclaimed. "The jinxer!"

Van looked, too, and for a while he was silent. Then he said, "I wonder what that fellow's up to. In fact, I'd like to follow him and find out. But I can't, doggone it! As soon as we let these beavers loose I gotta hightail it for Denver. There's a big meeting of Game and Fish people to make plans for the open season on mountain sheep this fall."

"You mean they are going to let hunters kill the sheep?" said Doc. "They're dying off already. There won't be any left."

"That's what *you* think," said Van. "We got a little scheme up our sleeves. The hunters will be doing the

sheep a great big favor." He chuckled to himself about
something. But he wouldn't say another word to the boys
about what the plan was.

Jay all the while had been keeping his eye on the man
with the box. The man now sat on a boulder as if he were
resting. He was so far away that it was hard to tell what
he looked like. Jay thought he must be a rather small
man.

"I have an idea," Jay suddenly said to Van. "Doc and
I have the whole day off. We could follow him and see
what he's up to."

"Your grandma would have a fit," Van said. "I told
her I'd bring you kids back as soon as we were done."

Jay put up an argument, and so did Doc. In the end
they convinced Van that nothing could happen to them.
They knew the country—they had been all over the area on
horseback in the last month.

Almost before the beavers stepped dazedly out of their
cage, the boys turned toward the mountainside. Stooping
low, they went under the sheltering branches of the quak-
ing aspen trees. The man with the box was out of sight
now, but they headed straight for the shoulder of rock
where he had been sitting.

Above the aspens, the mountain slope was covered for a long way with a thick stand of spruce. It made perfect cover for them, but the going was slow. Giant trees that had died and been blown over by furious mountain winds lay everywhere in the deep shade under the living evergreens. Doc was breathing heavily, but for once he did not ask Jay to let him "blow." He knew there would be time enough for that when they reached the burned-over area where they would be out in the open.

Soon they were almost there, and they stopped while they were still hidden under the dark, downward-sloping branches of the trees. Ahead was the stretch of devastated forest. Weathered tree trunks stood up like abandoned telephone poles. Shrubs and wild raspberry bushes grew here and there, waist high. The red ripe berries reminded Jay suddenly that it was past lunchtime.

A little rise in the land kept the boys from seeing the outcropping of rock they were headed for, but still they wanted to be careful. If they walked upright through the brush, the man with the box might see them. No telling which direction he might take. They would have to stoop down and scuttle from one clump of bushes to another, and they would have to be quiet. The wind was still, and the sound of the stream below had long since been left behind. There was none of the usual mountain murmur to conceal any noise they made.

Moving very cautiously, they approached the rise of land that would give them a view of the rock. They scarcely expected the man would be sitting there waiting for them, but there was no use taking chances. At the brow of the rise they had no cover except clumps of tall scarlet paintbrush. Jay lowered himself to his belly and wormed along until he could see the outcropping clearly. He peered ahead through the splashes of red flowers. There sat the man with the box. Jay could see that the fellow was small, just as he had thought. He wore blue jeans, a khaki jacket, and a Stetson. It was old and floppy, but somehow different from the Stetsons that a lot of mountain men wore.

The man was folding up a piece of waxed paper—the kind that sandwiches are wrapped in—and his jaws moved. Apparently he had just finished his lunch. Methodically he unfastened a canteen from his belt, shook it to see how much water was in it, and took three careful swallows. A moment later he rose, looked about, and neatly stuffed the paper in a crevice in the rock, then piled small stones over it so it would not blow away. This was no ordinary tenderfoot cluttering up the woods with his garbage.

Jay signaled for Doc to hug the earth as the man stretched and looked around. Suddenly Jay realized that the box lay on the ground at the stranger's feet. Now the man selected a patch of matted mountain grass and stretched out on it, with his hat tilted down over his eyes.

Jay crawled back to Doc and reported in a whisper, "The guy's going to take a nap. No telling how long we'll be stuck here. He was eating his lunch."

"Jeepers, I'm starved!" said Doc. "Got anything to eat?"

"Just a little chunk of bittersweet chocolate," Jay answered.

"Let's have it," said Doc. "Then we'll beat the birds to this raspberry patch. We'll have to fill up on berries."

Quietly they moved a little way down the slope and began picking berries, careful to keep low behind the brush.

"He sure doesn't act very crazy," Jay said. "He seems to know what he's doing—but what's he up to?"

"That's what we'll have to find out, even if it takes us the whole day," Doc answered. "Did you get a good look at the box?"

"Well, I could see it looked about as big as an oversized cornflakes box, but it was black, like leather or something. What do you suppose?"

"I suppose we better go back up and keep an eye on him," Doc answered. "In case he just takes a short beauty rest."

The two boys looked at each other and grinned. Their mouths were red from raspberry juice and their hands stained. Now both of them crawled through the paint brush to the top of the rise. The man was still flat on his back with his hat over his eyes. For long, tedious minutes the boys lay waiting. No telling how long the mysterious stranger would have stayed there resting, but suddenly he seemed bothered by something—maybe a bee. He sat up cautiously with his eye on whatever was buzzing around close to him. Finally he got up and made ready to leave.

Jay and Doc held their breath while the man turned toward the box. They could see it was heavy from the way he lifted it and adjusted the strap that held it over his shoulder. It seemed also that he was taking good care of the box; he didn't want to let it drop. With a feeling of dismay, the boys watched him turn and head up the mountain, straight up the burned-over area. This meant they would have to keep crouched behind shrubs if they wanted to follow him.

The forest fire that had burned through this place had apparently been driven by a narrow, rising current of wind that carried the blaze all the way to the last scraggly trees at timberline. It was hard work to walk crouched over —but worse than that, they would have a long wait if the man with the box hiked any distance above timberline. There the country was a kind of smooth wasteland called tundra, with a few scattered outcroppings of rock. The boys knew they would be seen if they emerged from the trees and tried to follow him. They would have to wait until he had crossed the ridge before they could move.

The man did just as they feared he would. Hiking easily and steadily in a way that showed he was in wonderful condition, his slight, wiry figure moved across the shelterless tundra. The boys crouched behind a dark, fantastic-shaped timberline tree. Scores of years of fierce Arctic winds had blown against the spruce and made it grow like a creeping thing along the ground. This was the last shelter they could see for about a quarter of a mile. Between them and the high horizon line were only two knobs of weathered rock sticking up from the monotonous tundra. The man with the box headed straight for the first of these knobs.

The boys saw his nimble legs in the distance scrambling over the parts of the rock not covered by grass and moss. He seemed to open the box and do something, but he was so far away that they couldn't tell what. He repeated this same performance at the second rock knob.

"What do you suppose he's doing?" Jay asked.

"I don't know. Do you think it's smart for us to go on?"

"Oh, sure. We're safe enough as long as he doesn't see us," Jay answered.

More than an hour passed before the man reached the horizon. Once he paused and looked upward. He stood motionless so long that the boys' eyes swept up the ridge to see what could be holding his attention.

"Lookit! Sheep—mountain sheep!" Doc said with sudden excitement. He pointed up the slope.

There, high above them, were the dirty remnants of a snowbank still left from last winter's blizzards. A hollowed-out place in the side of the mountain had sheltered the snow and kept it from melting. Below it the grass had grown thick and lush. No question about it—the sheep were there grazing.

"Van must have been kidding when he said that it

would be good for the sheep to have a hunting season," Jay said.

"No. I'm sure he meant it, but darned if I can figure out why," Doc replied. "You know what? I'm going to put in for a license to hunt them."

"What!" Jay exclaimed with a grin. "And take another hike up this way? Pretty soon you're going to forget how to ride a horse."

Just then something startled the sheep and they bounded away from the base of the snowbank and circled out of sight toward rocky ledges higher up.

The man with the box moved on. Soon he disappeared over the horizon. Apparently he was not going to climb higher along the treeless ridge but was headed down toward North Fork Canyon.

"Come on, let's go after him," Jay said, relieved to get up and move once more.

Hiking as fast as they could in the thin mountain air, they approached the first knob of rock where the man had stopped. But look as they would, they could find nothing that was a clue of any sort. There was nothing at the second rock outcropping either. Although they were only walking, their lungs heaved as if they had gone at a fast run.

Jay now stopped at frequent intervals to "blow." Each time, Doc was ready to go on with the pursuit as soon as Jay was. He had come this far and he hated to lose the man's trail.

At the point where they had last seen the man, they began to move cautiously. The rounded shape of the tundra kept them from looking very far ahead. Soon, however, they saw him striding steadily down toward timberline on the side of North Fork Canyon.

"He seems to know where he's going, but darned if I do," Jay remarked.

"Let's see," Doc said. "I don't think there's anything down there except an old abandoned mine shaft. It goes straight down for about thirty feet. Dad and I were scared our cattle would fall into it so we tore down an old shed and built a fence around the hole."

After the man disappeared into the trees, Jay and Doc ran down the long slope. It would be safe to follow him closer in the shelter of the trees. Soon after they reached the low timberline growth, Jay stepped out on a jutting ledge of rock, then jumped back.

"He's right down there," he whispered to Doc. "Be careful." He crouched on his hands and knees and crawled back again to the ledge. Doc crawled beside him.

"That's the old mine shaft I was telling you about," Doc said quietly.

There, a couple of hundred yards below in a clearing among the trees, stood a crude fence made of weathered boards and timbers. The man with the box had crawled through the fence and was standing half-concealed at the edge of the mine shaft. They could see him take the box off his shoulder. For a minute his hands were busy at something. Then he lay down on his belly near the edge of the shaft and slowly lowered the box into the mine by a cord he had obviously tied to it.

"Gee, maybe he's going to hide that thing there. If he does, we can sure find out what it is when he leaves," Doc said excitedly.

But they soon had to give up all thought of examining the box. The man pulled it back up, slung it on his shoulder again, and was soon lost to view in the dense spruce forest.

"Doggone!" Jay said. "Well, let's get a move on. We got to be as quiet as we can."

"I don't know about that," Doc answered. "The open places from here on down will have some of our cattle in

them. They make a heck of a racket when they step on broken branches. That guy is sure to know the cattle are here, and he'll think any noise we make comes from them."

Every once in a while now they caught sight of movement ahead. The first time it was the brown hide of a Circle M steer. But again and again they saw the khaki windbreaker and blue jeans that told them they were still on the trail. A few hundred yards from the bottom of the canyon, the man swung sharply left onto the faint tracks of an old wagon road.

"Hey!" Jay exclaimed. "That road goes to the old Doubtful Mine. Do you suppose he's going to drop his box down again? No, he couldn't. That mine shaft goes straight into the mountain. Come on, let's see what he does."

Keeping off the open road, Jay and Doc scrambled through the trees until the yellow-gray mine dump appeared just ahead. Beside it stood a shack. Between the shack and the dump lay a patch of thick green grass, watered by the trickle from a spring somewhere deep in the old mine. Half a dozen Circle M steers were grazing peacefully on the grass.

Suddenly the placid animals were startled by a loud yell—

and so were Doc and Jay.

"Get out! Beat it! Scram!" the wiry little man shouted at them.

Then the boys saw him pick up small stones from the dump and throw them in the direction of the cattle. A moment later the steers turned and lumbered off into the brush.

"Look at that!" Doc said. "He's the one that's been stampeding our cattle. Doggone it, if he makes one of them break a leg running through fallen timber—"

But the man did not take up the chase. Instead he turned toward the old cabin, stood by the door for a moment while he fumbled in his pocket. Then, unlocking a shiny new padlock, he opened the door and went in. He was out again in a moment, without his box, but carrying an ax in his hand.

At the sound of chopping behind the cabin, Doc said, "He must be living here."

"I guess so," Jay said. "You've been range riding up here this summer. Didn't you see any signs of him then?"

"No," Doc admitted. "But then I wasn't looking for anybody."

The boys sat and thought for a while. Suddenly they

realized they were a long way from home and the sun was getting low. They weren't sure they wanted to walk in and get acquainted with this strange fellow. Not right now, anyhow. If they hurried down to Lucky Lake, they might just be able to hitch a ride with some tourist returning from a day's fishing. Another day they would find out more about the man with the box—the man who yelled at cows.

## CHAPTER 13 ... Human Beaver Bait

Jay was weary. He let Maude go at as slow a pace as the tired horse wanted. Even Doc sat relaxed in the saddle, and the lean-muscled legs of Buck moved slowly. Benzy alone seemed to have some energy to spare. All day long for the last three days the boys had been rounding up Circle M cattle. Each day they penned a bunch of the steers in a corral near the road, then helped load the animals into a truck that took them down to the feeding lot in the valley near Fremont.

Jay watched Benzy, still zigzagging from the woods on one side of the road to the woods on the other. He wondered how the little dog could still make the effort. Suddenly Benzy stopped and looked ahead with interest. In another moment Jay was off his horse. There, parked beside the road just ahead, was the blue station wagon which, he knew, belonged to Jerrold George III. Its tailgate was open invitingly, and so was one of the side doors. Jay felt in no mood to have Benzy swipe anything more from that car.

"Come here, you low-down, thieving, underslung Indian gopher hound," he whispered to the dog. "Come back here, Benzy."

With obvious reluctance, the dog obeyed and came to Jay. In another moment Jay was back up in the saddle, holding Benzy across his lap.

"I don't want you messing around with Jerrold the Third this time," Jay muttered. "You're going to get a free ride for a while."

"I wonder what his Royal Highness is doing here," Doc said.

"Fishing probably," Jay answered. "The beaver ponds along here are pretty well stocked."

The horses began to shuffle forward, choosing to walk in the soft low grass beside the road. As they came close to the parked blue station wagon, Jay gave a perfunctory glance down the gentle slope at the right toward one of the ponds. Then he reined in and whispered to Doc, "Pipe that!"

There, on a sunny open patch of grass near the shore

of the pond, was a sight that spread grins over the weary faces of both boys. Dressed in fancy dude costumes, Mr. George, his wife, and two strangers lay stretched out in the sun, each one on a bright-colored rubber air mattress. They all wore dark sun glasses and seemed determined to get a deep coat of tan. Behind them, placed carefully against a folding aluminum camp table, were four elegant fishing rods.

The two boys looked at each other and shook with silent belly-laughs. Summer folks were usually good for laughs of one kind or another, but this was the best yet.

Apparently none of the sun-bathers had heard the horses. They might even have been asleep. At any rate, they rested peacefully in the gaudiest collection of outdoor costumes Doc and Jay had ever seen. The two boys looked contentedly at their own dirty jeans and work-soiled shirts and decided to move on.

"Just a minute!" Doc whispered. "Look there!"

Emerging from the aspen grove above the pond and waddling purposefully toward the sun-bathers was a sleek, full-grown beaver. Instead of skirting around the prone figures, the beaver headed straight toward Mrs. George who was nearest him. On and on he came, while the two boys sat and watched in silent fascination. The beaver did not stop or hesitate. He sniffed up close to her purple shirt and finally stuck his muzzle almost into her ear.

Letting out a shriek, Mrs. George jumped up, tore off her glasses, and tumbled backward over the other three people. Benzy, who had been bored and tired, hadn't noticed the approach of the beaver. But the shriek electrified him into action. With an eel-like motion, he slithered out of Jay's lap, tobogganed down his leg, and ran off toward the excitement. In another moment he was in hot pursuit of the retreating beaver.

"It was going to bite me!" Mrs. George yelled, over and over.

Her husband untangled himself from the brilliant-hued mass of summer people. Seeing the beaver with Benzy in pursuit, he shouted, "Sic him! Sic him!"

The beaver reached the water just ahead of the short-legged dog. But the water didn't stop Benzy. With a yip, he plunged in and paddled frantically, trying to keep up with the frightened beaver. Soon the beaver seemed to realize that he was safe now in his own element. Instead of heading for the shelter of his own lodge, he swam around the pond as if he were leading Benzy a chase for the fun

of it. Occasionally he would disappear, swim underwater, and then come up behind Benzy.

Doc was laughing so hard he had to get off his horse. Between helpless gasps of merriment, he managed to warn Jay, "You better get the pooch back. Beavers *can* get mad at a dog and use their teeth. If this one should, then it's good-by Benzy."

Jay rode down to the edge of the pond and tried to get Benzy's attention. Whether he succeeded or not was anybody's guess. All of a sudden, the dog turned, swam rapidly to the bank, and ran to the excited group of people. Then, right in their midst, he shook himself with lusty abandon, spraying water all over immaculate silk shirts and neatly creased slacks.

Benzy had done it again! Jay had the distinct feeling that the time had come for him to depart. He jumped off his horse and picked the dog up. Benzy, full of the joy of life after his refreshing swim, almost squirmed up out of Jay's arms as he affectionately licked his master's face.

Mrs. George was still repeating, "He tried to bite me! He did! That beaver attacked me! Jerrold, why don't you shoot it?"

This was almost more than Doc could stand. He shook

with half-controlled laughter, then said to Jay between chuckles, "Did you smell that beaver bait?" He jerked his head toward Mrs. George.

Now a great light dawned on Jay. He turned his back on the group to conceal a new outburst of guffaws.

Doc somehow felt he owed it to the beaver to explain. "Look, Mrs. George," he said, "I want to ask you something. Haven't you got perfume on?"

The lady stopped her frantic noise as suddenly as she had begun.

"Young man, whatever do you mean?" she asked haughtily.

"Well, there's stuff in perfume that's the same as the stuff they put in beaver bait. A beaver just naturally can't keep away from it. That little fellow wasn't trying to bite you. He just liked your smell."

"Jerrold!" Mrs. George exclaimed. "Did you ever hear such impertinent nonsense!"

"It honestly isn't nonsense," Jay put in quickly. "Mr. Hollister—he's the beaver conservation man—he told us all about it. He said that beavers will follow ladies who wear strong perfume. He has even seen it happen."

Mrs. George looked more angry and flustered than ever.

"Doc, we better get out of here," Jay said, still trying to control Benzy. He held the dog under his left arm and hoisted himself awkwardly into the saddle.

"What a nasty little animal," he heard Mrs. George mutter as he rode away. "Water all over!"

"Some of these summer folks are lulus!" said Doc. "Wait till we tell Van."

Even Buck and Maude seemed somewhat cheered up by the episode. They broke into a mild trot as they neared the grassy edge of Lucky Lake. The boys turned off the road and went toward an opening in the trees where they had a tent and bedrolls. This would be the third night that they had camped here during the roundup. They had hoped to go home tonight, but four steers were missing from the herd they had finally brought down from the range. Cattle trucks had already taken away the ninety animals they had hazed in during the three days they had been working. Now the boys had to hunt for the missing four. It might be very tough work. No telling where the animals were hiding out.

After they had watered the horses and hobbled them in a small patch of mountain grass, Jay built a campfire while Doc opened some cans of food. They were busy stuffing themselves with hot pork and beans when a voice suddenly surprised them.

"Got any more grub?" It was Ashy.

"Sure. Help yourself," Jay answered. "If there's not enough in the pot, I'll open you another can."

"Coming up from Payrock this afternoon, I met your father hauling out cattle," Ashy said to Doc. "Aren't you early this year?"

"Yep," Doc answered. "More than a week. But Dad didn't want to take any chances. Say! I guess you haven't heard. We saw that crazy fellow with a box. Jay and I followed him for quite a while. We caught him chasing the cattle."

"I thought he was the guy," Ashy grunted.

The boys went on and told him the whole story. Although Doc's father didn't really believe in jinxes, and although he hadn't seen any real proof that the man with the box was causing stampedes on purpose, still his cattle were valuable, and he decided to get them down to the valley a little early.

"We found out where that crazy guy's living, too," Jay said. "In the old cabin by the mouth of the Doubtful Mine."

"At least he *was*," Doc added. "We didn't see him at all

during the roundup these last few days."

"That's because he was over on the Middle Fork," said Ashy. "I saw him there yesterday and the day before. He was all over the place with that box of his."

"What do you figure the box is for?" Jay asked.

"What's anything for that a crazy man does?" Ashy retorted.

"Say, Ashy, did you put in for a license to hunt mountain sheep?" Doc asked, as the old man got to his feet and prepared to leave in his usual unceremonious way.

"What's that?"

"Didn't you know there's going to be an open season on bighorn rams?" said Doc.

"There hasn't been a season for sixty years," said Ashy. "No sense in having one now. They're dying off!"

"That's what I told Van. But he says there's a reason for the open season. He wouldn't tell what it was. Anyway, you write in and ask for the license. If too many people write in, they'll draw lots and pick just a certain number that'll be allowed to hunt here in the Payrock country."

"Humph!" Ashy said.

"You can only shoot the old rams," Jay added. "I sure wish I knew how shooting the old rams would cure the lung disease."

"Is that what Van said?" the old man asked sharply. But without waiting for an answer, he shouldered his pack and was gone up the trail toward his cabin.

## CHAPTER 14 ... The Blasted Cabin

"There's only one thing I can think of," Doc said to Jay. "Those four pesky steers probably don't mind the cold nights as much as the rest of the critters. They must be grazing on the good grass way up on the range above where we've looked—unless, of course, the jinx got 'em."

All day yesterday the two boys had scoured the lower part of the range looking for the four missing steers. Their horses were tired. They had had no time off since the roundup began four days ago.

"Let's follow the old mining road up the North Fork all the way to timberline," Jay suggested. "The road will be easier on Buck and Maude. Then when we get to Ute Point we'll have a good view of the whole canyon. We might just be lucky enough to spot the steers from there."

Doc agreed, and by ten o'clock they were standing on

the barren ledge called Ute Point. They had left their
horses to rest and graze in an open spot below the point,
and Benzy had stayed with the animals, stretched out on
a warm rock for a nap. Studying each break in the trees
below them, the boys looked hopefully for any spot of
reddish brown and white that was in motion. It was worth
staying here for an hour or two even, instead of plunging
through the forest below where they could see only yards
ahead.

For a long time they discovered nothing. Jay grew restless. He turned and gave a great sweeping glance toward
the peaks of the Continental Divide that stood to the west.
Stubborn resentment filled him. These doggone cattle had
kept him from taking the hikes up here that he had looked
forward to all summer.

Of course, Jay thought to himself, he needed the money
that Mr. Martin was paying him for his help with the
roundup. High school would start the day after Labor
Day, and there were a lot of things he had to buy. Only
four days were left between now and the opening of school,
when he would move down to the plains to live on the
Martin ranch near Fremont. Every minute of these last
precious days would be filled. Even if he and Doc found

the cattle today, he was way behind in his chores at the store. He had to get everything shipshape for Grandma, because he would be coming up to Payrock only on week ends and for holidays during the winter. He looked at the peaks one by one and thought of the climbs he had planned to make there this summer. He hadn't been able to make a one of them. So many things had happened since the day he saw the parachuting beavers. Even his hiking plans seemed to be jinxed.

For a moment Jay's eyes rested on the rough, enormous shape of Comanche Peak, his favorite. If the weather stayed open, maybe he could make that climb the first week end after school started. Or maybe he could get Ken Schultz and some of the Rescue Squad people to let him go on a trip with them. As he studied the sheer north face of the peak, looking for possible ways to go up with climbing equipment, he caught a fleck of motion on the ridge between him and the peak. Something moved again. Then there were several separate bits of motion.

"Look over there, Doc," Jay said. "Bighorns again."

"Uh-huh, I bet that's the same band we saw across the canyon the other day. I sure hope I'm one of the lucky ones that gets a license to hunt 'em. As long as it's legal,

I'd sure like to have a big old ram's head stuffed and hanging in my room."

"You're going to have some hike sneaking up on them, that's all I've got to say," Jay commented, studying the gray-brown figures in the distance.

For half an hour they looked by turns down the canyon for cattle and up the mountain at the sheep. Slowly the sheep grazed closer and closer. At last they were near enough so that their outlines could be seen clearly.

"If we stay real quiet, maybe they'll come almost up to us," Doc whispered. "Dad says it's happened to him. They're not scared of people because they haven't been hunted for so many years."

Fascinated, the boys waited, almost forgetting the cattle. Now they could actually make out the mournful, ashen-colored faces of the beasts.

Doc studied them intently, and at last he said in dismay. "Look at their horns."

"What about them?" Jay whispered back.

"There's not an old ram among them. Look at those three that have curling horns. Their horns aren't half grown. That means they're too young to shoot." The dozen other full-grown sheep in the band all had horn

that were nearly straight, slanting back from their fore-
heads instead of curling around at the side of their heads.
These were ewes.

"Don't you see, dopey?" said Doc. "What's the use of
getting a hunting license if there aren't any old rams to
hunt? You can tell an old ram because his horns curl forward and get to be three feet or so long."

"Maybe they all died of lung disease," said Jay.

"If that's so, there would be no sense in having an open
season," Doc answered. "I give up. We'll ask Van."

"Hey, we can't stay here all day," Jay said suddenly. "We
better get a move on."

Reluctantly Doc turned to have another look down the
valley. Jay stretched his legs and started to stand up. The
sudden motion startled the always-watchful sheep, and
in a moment they were gone.

But the long wait on Ute Point had not been wasted.
They looked down again into the canyon bottom, and there
they saw the patch of red-brown and white they had been
searching for. A steer moved across an open spot in the
forest below. Perhaps the others were nearby.

A few minutes of quick riding ended their worries. The
missing cattle were close together, and soon the boys had

them ambling down the old mine road.

When they reached the place where there was a turn-off to the cabin at the Doubtful Mine, Jay said, "Let's just ride up and see what we can see." Somehow, being on horseback, he had a sense of confidence he had lacked when he and Doc tracked the man with the box. Anyway, there wasn't any reason why a couple of cowhands shouldn't drop in and ask for a drink from the man's spring.

The cattle were headed peacefully down the old road, and Doc knew they couldn't get far away, so he agreed.

Buck, tough mountain pony that he was, made better time up the steep road than Maude could. Jay saw Doc start to go around the curve onto the top of the mine dump. Then Doc suddenly pulled in his horse and waited. Jay soon found out why he had stopped. The cabin door was swinging open, its glass panes broken. The padlock, still fastened, dangled from the hasp as if the whole thing had been ripped loose from the door jamb.

The boys sat still for a minute, then dismounted and walked hesitantly toward the weathered board shack. The windowpane was broken, too. They peered through the door. Everything inside was a mass of wreckage.

Jay let out a low whistle. "Looks like that guy really did

go plumb loony. Everything in the place is smashed to pieces."

Doc stopped and picked up an aluminum coffeepot. "Look at that! He was even shooting holes in this thing." Broken dishes, pieces of glass lampshade, and bits of iron littered the floor.

Benzy ran everywhere in a frenzy of delight, wrestling with torn bits of clothing.

"My gosh, he took his ax and smashed his stove to pieces!" Jay exclaimed.

"And look at that—he even smashed out the boards in the end wall. Were we ever right that he's crazy! Maybe we better get out."

But Jay had been puzzling over the broken bits of stove. It had been smashed into a thousand small pieces. Even with a sledge hammer a man would have had an awful job pounding the cast iron into such little bits. Then Jay's curious eyes moved from the place where the stove had sat to the wall behind and up to the ceiling. He swept a glance around the whole room.

"I got it!" he cried excitedly. "This place was dynamited! Somebody must have put dynamite in the stove and then set it off. There are chunks of stove stuck in the ceiling. It wasn't bullets—it was pieces of stove that hit the coffeepot!"

In an awed voice Doc murmured, "Maybe the crazy guy blew himself up!"

Jay shuddered and shut his eyes. He had visions of finding odd fingers and splotches of blood. But when he opened his eyes, there was not a sign of bones or flesh.

"At least he wasn't inside when the dynamite went off," Jay said in relief.

"I know one thing—I'm getting out," Doc said. "We better go home and phone the sheriff about this."

## CHAPTER 15 . . . "Crazy"

Jay fidgeted. He had been sitting on the platform of the loading corral for an hour. It would be another hour, maybe two, before the truck came to pick up the four steers that had wasted so much of Jay's time. In a few more days summer would be over, and half of the things he had wanted to accomplish remained undone.

He had taken only a few hikes. He had been back to see the black beavers only once. He was no closer to finding the jinx of Payrock Canyon than he had been in the middle of the summer. As he thought over all the queer events of the last few weeks, everything seemed to point toward the man with the box. And now dynamite had blown to smithereens all chances of finding out any more about the man.

Jay was even annoyed at Doc. He seemed to get all the

pleasure he needed just riding his buckskin pony. Anything else that happened, like seeing black beavers or mountain sheep, was so much extra good luck to Doc. He didn't even get fighting mad about the jinx on the Circle M cattle. Right now he was perfectly happy sitting on a rock by the creek watching a water ouzel bob up and down. The little gray bird sang lustily at times, and once in a while it dove under the surface of a rocky pool where it actually swam underwater with a flying motion of its wings.

Come to think of it, Jay realized, he was also irritated with Benzy. The little dog was perfectly happy chasing ground squirrels. Nobody but Jay seemed to care that the precious summer was gone, with no way of getting it back.

Suddenly a noise on the road made Jay look up. There, coming down from the direction of Lucky Lake, was a shiny sedan with the oversized aerial and spotlight on the top that marked it as Sheriff Bert McKenney's car. In a moment it had pulled up by the loading platform.

"Hi, Bert," Jay called.

Doc came up from the creek as the sheriff called out lazily, "Nice day for the race."

Doc was off guard for the moment. "What race?" he asked with a mild show of interest.

"The human race," the sheriff answered with a grin. It always pleased him when he found someone who hadn't heard his threadbare joke before.

"You win on that one," Doc said good-naturedly.

Jay snapped out of his end-of-summer doldrums suddenly. "Hey, Bert! We were going to phone you," he said.

"That so?"

"Yeah—we found that old cabin up at the Doubtful Mine all blown to smithereens."

"The jinxer was living there," Doc put in.

"The *who?*" said Bert.

"The man with the box," Jay hastened to explain. "The crazy guy that's been up here this summer. We followed him to the cabin the other day. We went back today to see what we could find out about him, and everything was a mess. It looked like somebody put dynamite in the stove and blew it sky high."

"Yeah, I know," said Bert casually. "I've seen it."

Jay was surprised and a little irritated. He didn't like the way the sheriff always seemed to know everything—or at least pretended he did.

"You've seen it?"

"I got a call this morning," the sheriff answered. "The

fellow who is closing up Camp Wapiti phoned me about it. So I took a run up to look things over."

The boys listened with growing excitement to the sheriff's story. The man with the box had appeared yesterday evening at Camp Wapiti. He wasn't a stranger there, although the camp manager didn't know him well. The man had been in and out of camp all summer, because he was a friend of the owner. In fact, the owner got all the man's supplies for him and brought them up in the camp truck.

"So that's why he never came to the store!" Jay exclaimed. "But what was he supposed to be doing up here?"

"Prospecting for uranium," the sheriff answered. "He walked around with his Geiger counter, hoping to strike it rich. That's what the fellow at Wapiti told me."

"Geiger counter! Do you suppose that's what he had in the box?"

"Must have been," the sheriff said. Then he added, "I'm kinda sore about him. I came all the way up here on purpose to get his story. But he'd lit out."

Bert went on with the story he had heard from the camp manager. Last night the man with the box just asked if he could spend the night at Wapiti. He had often done this. Then this morning, after he had got a new supply of food, he asked the manager for a sleeping bag and more supplies. He said almost everything he owned had been blown up yesterday in the cabin where he was staying. He told of coming back from a prospecting trip with his Geiger counter on the Middle Fork of Payrock Creek and finding that somebody had set off a blast of dynamite.

The manager was scared. If somebody was dynamiting buildings, they might go after Camp Wapiti next. So he called the sheriff. But before the manager knew it, the man with the box had packed up and gone. He was a queer kind of lonely duck. The only thing he said was that he planned to try his luck over across the Continental Divide, in Devil's Crater.

"Something about this sure sounds fishy," Jay commented. "Ashy says that guy is nuts. He must be, if he goes off alone like that. . . . Why, he might have been blown up himself."

"What are you going to do about it?" Doc asked the sheriff.

"There's nothing much I can do," the sheriff answered. "I went up to the Doubtful and looked the place over. The only clue was the fresh track of a couple of horses that the dynamiters might have been riding."

"Hey, you don't suspect we did it, do you?" Doc asked with some worry in his voice. "Those were our horses."

"I reckon I ought to search your packs to see if you got any caps or fuse," the sheriff said importantly.

Jay wasn't sure whether or not Bert was joking. "Say, we can prove we weren't anywhere near that cabin yesterday."

"How?" the sheriff asked.

"That's right," Doc said. "We were looking for these four steers, and we didn't get 'em yesterday. It was today we got them, up the North Fork above the Doubtful cabin."

"Can you prove it?" the sheriff asked.

"Sure," said Doc. "Jay will swear to it, and so will I."

"You guys better not grow up to be lawyers," the sheriff said. "Who do you have to prove you weren't there yesterday—nothing but four steers that you didn't catch until today." Then he slapped his thigh and chuckled. "Take it easy. I guess you wouldn't do a trick like that. But I sure wish I knew who did."

Jay was angry. Bert had halfway suspected him and Doc. But Jay decided it might not be smart to show his annoyance. The sheriff might get really suspicious. Instead, Jay said, "You know what? I bet that fellow blew up the cabin himself. Then he cleared out because he didn't want to see you, Bert. If a man is nuts, he does things like that."

"I doubt it," the sheriff said. "Anyway, we should get some line on him in a few days. I phoned the sheriff over in Bridger County. When that fellow comes down out of Devil's Crater into Humboldt where he said he was going to pick up his mail, he'll have a lot of questions to answer."

The sheriff started his car. "Let me know if you hear of any more monkeyshines around here," he called. "Be seeing you." And he waved as he drove off down the road.

"Uranium! Boy!" Doc exclaimed. "Do you suppose we could find some? Maybe we ought to have a Geiger counter ourselves to carry around while we're riding the range."

But Jay was thinking about something else. Now he understood why the man with the box had scrambled around over outcroppings of rock the day the boys followed him, and why he had lowered his box into the old mine shaft. The fellow was trying everywhere to find the magic mineral that could lead him to great wealth.

"I wonder how a Geiger counter works," Jay said.

"By telepathy," Doc answered with a grin. "It just begins buzzing all by itself whenever it comes close to a bed of rock that's got some uranium ore in it."

Two more cars drove by, and the boys kept wishing that the cattle truck would come. Then a battered old jalopy appeared from the direction of Lucky Lake.

"Hi, Jay. Hi, Doc," the driver called, and a pair of thick eyeglasses appeared around the side of the windshield. It was Ken Schultz.

"What you doing up here?" Jay asked. "Another rescue?"

"No, some of us were just practicing on a hypothetical rescue problem," Ken answered.

"You mean you were doing the kind of thing you do in your climbing classes?" Jay asked with real interest.

"Well, sort of," said Ken. "The four of us who went today will all be teachers in the classes. We just wanted to get the cricks out of our joints."

"Do you suppose there's a chance I could go to those classes? Or do you only take college students?" Ever since the night of the rescue of the red-headed twins, Jay had been thinking about the climbing school. Somehow he had convinced himself that it would be almost impossible for a lowly high school sophomore to get into a school run for college students. It had even seemed almost impossible to find out whether there was a chance for him. Now, with

a direct question, he had leaped a great hurdle that had been in his mind. And it all seemed so obvious and simple when Ken answered:

"Sure, come ahead. We'll be glad to have you."

Suddenly all of Jay's bleak thoughts about the summer disappointments vanished from his mind. He found himself looking forward to winter with the keenest interest. He would be learning all the latest techniques of rock climbing and search and rescue work. Maybe he could even join the Rescue Squad itself.

"How about you, Doc? Do you want to join the class, too?" Ken asked.

Doc looked startled and uncertain.

Jay said joshingly, "Have you got special classes to teach horses how to climb, Ken? Doc would like to ride his horse to school."

"Aw, cut that corny stuff," Doc replied. "I guess I showed you I can hike as well as anybody."

Then more seriously Jay said, "It wouldn't hurt you to join the class and have a few lessons before you go on the bighorn hunt—if you get a license."

"Did you put in for a license?" Ken asked with interest. "I didn't know you were old enough."

"Sure, you only have to be fifteen," Doc answered. "Van Hollister told me. I wouldn't want to go much, except that Van said the hunting season would be good for the sheep."

"I'm going along with him, just for company," Jay said. "Say, that gives me an idea, Ken. Why don't you come, too? *If* he gets a license."

"Not a bad idea," Ken answered. "Where are you going?"

"Up in the Comanche Peak area," said Doc. "There's a band of sheep up there. We've seen some of them, and there must be some old bighorn rams around."

"I didn't see any sheep today. I was up there, as a matter of fact. But, of course, that doesn't prove anything," said Ken. "They might have got scared away by a fellow we saw way ahead of us."

Jay perked up. "Was the fellow by any chance carrying a box?" he asked.

"Yeah, that's right, he had a big pack and some kind of box," Ken answered. "You know him?"

"Do we know him!" Jay said. And then he and Doc told Ken the whole story.

When they had finished, Ken said, "It's a downright shame the way these uranium prospectors are wasting their time. Any geologist at the college could tell them there's not a bit of the ore in this whole area. But the woods are full of prospectors, and every single one of these get-rich-quick experts thinks he's the only prospector in the hills. I never saw one yet that didn't act as secretive as if he was on the trail of Captain Kidd's buried treasure."

"Are you *sure* there's no uranium here?" Jay asked.

"You probably don't remember," Ken answered, "but a few years ago the government sent geologists with Geiger counters over every inch of this territory. They didn't find a thing." After a pause Ken went on. "Another thing that riles me. Sooner or later the Rescue Squad is going to get called out to help one of those prospectors out of some fix he's got into. Most of them don't know a thing about the mountains. Take the man we saw today."

Jay broke in, "That fellow's a good hiker. We ought to know. We trailed him."

"He may have a good pair of legs and good lungs," Ken replied. "But he's soft in the head."

"That's what we told you," said Doc. "He's crazy as a loon."

"I'm not talking about all this jinx stuff," Ken answered. "Nobody, I don't care who it is, should hike in this country alone. If you do, I still say you're soft in the head. Anything could happen, and if you're alone there's nobody to help you. Take this fellow. He was going toward Devil's Crater. That's the worst country in seven counties. Bad weather may break any day now. If he sprained his ankle he could get caught in a storm above timberline and freeze to death. I'd have warned him about it today, but he had crossed the Divide before we could reach him."

"He sure is crazy," Jay said thoughtfully.

As Ken drove away, Doc called, "Don't forget. We've got a date for the bighorn hunt."

"*If* you get a license," Jay reminded him.

## CHAPTER 16 ... The Hunt Begins

Jay could hardly believe it when Doc did get his license. Even now, with the beginning of the bighorn hunt only a few hours away, it still seemed incredible.

Jay looked across the campfire and saw that Doc hadn't yet finished his beefsteak and buns, while Jay and Ken were already through with the apple pie that Grandma Himrod had baked for them. In the flickering light of their campfire, lines of worry showed on Doc's usually cheerful face.

"What's on your mind?" Jay finally asked him.

"Nothing. Why should there be?" was Doc's almost cross reply.

Now Jay was sure that Doc was troubled about something, but he would just have to wait until Doc came out with it. Jay walked over to Ken's car and took from the back seat a high-powered game rifle. The rifle belonged to Van Hollister who had offered to lend it to Doc as soon as the papers carried news that Doc had been one of the applicants lucky enough to get a bighorn hunting license. Pointing the gun carefully away from the fire, Jay tried to look through the telescopic sights. He wondered whether Doc might be worried about the gun. His friend was a crack shot with a .22, but Van had given him only a few lessons in using this rifle with its telescopic sights.

"Are you onto the tricks of this baby?" Jay asked.

"I'm not worried about the rifle. It's a beaut," Doc answered. "But I don't know about something else. What's the best way to hunt mountain sheep?"

Jay was surprised. "Didn't Van tell you?"

"I thought he did," Doc answered. "He said to keep using the field glasses and then when I saw sheep to sneak up on them, always keeping out of sight. He also said to start in at the salt lick on Comanche Peak and keep working north. That way there would be no other hunters in the area except Ashy, so it would be safe. The important thing, he said, was to keep going north. Ashy is supposed to go south."

"Well?" Jay said.

"Well, that's not enough to know about hunting," Doc answered. "I just suddenly thought—we don't know what's the best part of the sheep to aim at. We don't know *how* you're supposed to sneak up on them. I thought of everything else except that, doggone it."

Jay realized that Doc was right. They had the legal tag to put on the animal when they got it. Their packs were light, so Jay could carry Doc's bedroll as well as his own. In case Doc shot a ram, he could use his own packboard for carrying the head. They had a flour sack in which to bring home the animal's heart and liver and some of the meat. The boys had even sharpened their hunting knives. They thought they were prepared for everything.

"If I were you, Doc," Ken said judicially, "I wouldn't worry too much. You know as much as anybody does about bighorns. The fact is, nobody around here has hunted them for sixty years. Chances are even Ashy doesn't know any more than you do."

"One other thing, Van said," Doc recalled, "the ewes and the old rams will probably be in separate bunches at this time of the year. But he didn't say just how far apart they would be."

"Stop worrying," Jay advised him.

Everything was set for a quick getaway the next morning. Still nobody felt ready for sleep. The fire was there, definite and warm, but Jay and Doc weren't too sure about the warmth of the featherweight sleeping bags that Ken had borrowed for them from the Rescue Squad. Almost unconsciously they kept putting off the time when they would crawl into the flimsy-looking envelopes of nylon and eiderdown. As they delayed, they kept wondering, *Exactly how do you hunt mountain sheep?*

The two boys pondered in silence, while Ken turned on his flashlight and checked over the mountain-climbing gear he had brought along. This certainly didn't look like hunters' equipment to Jay. He could imagine the snorts that Ashy or the other oldtimers would give if they saw it. Actually, Jay didn't care if they got a sheep, so long as he had a chance to practice with some of Ken's stuff. There was a hundred and twenty-foot coil of light nylon rope and a much smaller coil of nylon cord.

A small canvas bag jingled metallically as Ken lifted it. Out of it came pitons, a special-shaped piton hammer, and a couple of things Jay had never seen before. They were made of metal and looked like shoe soles, with heavy spikes on the bottom, and straps attached.

"What do you call those things?" Jay asked Ken.

"Crampons," Ken explained. "You strap them onto your boots if you're going across ice. The spikes keep you from slipping. I brought my ice ax, too, just in case we have to go across a glacier."

Doc was interested in the equipment, but finally he yawned and said, "I guess I'd better try out that tissue-paper bedroll I'm going to sleep in—*you* think."

"You'll be surprised," Ken said. And the two boys were.

Each of them kicked a shallow trench in the sod to make a resting place for his hips. Then, using boots for pillows, they wiggled into the narrow envelopes.

"Hey, this is the nuts," Jay said appreciatively after a few moments of warming up.

"I've slept out in midwinter in one of these bags," Ken said, "and it kept me perfectly comfortable."

As Doc lay flat on his back in his bag, he looked up at the brilliant stars overhead, and he wondered where mountain sheep sleep at night. Or if they slept. Did they lie down or stand up? Did they huddle together for warmth?

Next morning, the three of them were up and on the trail before it was fully light. They wore pack boards to which their bedrolls and food for two days were neatly

lashed. Ken, in the lead, used his ice ax as a walking stick. Doc carried the rifle slung by its strap from his shoulder. To equalize the loads, Jay carried some of Doc's food and Ken's field glasses.

In a little while they passed Ashy's cabin and saw that the door was padlocked.

"You have to get up early to be ahead of that old fellow," Ken said. "He's already out on the trail. You know, it's a darn wonder that something hasn't happened to him, hiking around the way he does alone all the time."

"He knows too much about the mountains to get into any trouble," Jay said.

"I don't care," Ken answered. "Just by the law of averages he's going to wish he had help some day."

Jay and Doc looked at each other and grinned. Silently they agreed that Ken was an okay guy, but he sometimes got too preachy.

Before they reached timberline, Ken, who was in the lead, called a halt.

"I have a plan to suggest," he said. "Let's work this hunt the way we do a rescue mission. We'll make a search line through the trees—just in case the sheep have come down off the rocks to feed. Jay, you go off to the right. I'll go to the left. Doc can have the trail. We'll work in a slanting path up to timberline. That will bring us out just below the place where the salt lick is. We'll keep close enough together so we can yell for help if we have to. The big idea is to shove the sheep up above timberline where Doc can see them."

Soon the three of them were fanned out under the brilliant autumn gold of the aspens. They moved steadily up the mountain. Jay followed a low dyke of rock that ran up the ridge. This seemed the most likely route for sheep to take if they were coming down off the tundra into the trees.

Suddenly Jay's eyes picked up a bloody mess in an open spot ahead. Bits of fur and a rabbit head were all that remained of some animal's recent meal. The kill had been made this morning, Jay figured, perhaps only half an hour ago. He wondered whether it was a coyote or a wildcat that had caught the rabbit. Or perhaps a sleek brown marten had leaped down out of the spruce trees to nab its breakfast. The dry, gravelly earth was disturbed, but no clear tracks remained.

Jay went on up the steep slope. Ahead he saw a scraggly line of willows only waist high, marking a spring. Possibly the sheep had been here, and there would be tracks. Pushing through the bare branches of the willow shrubs, he studied the moist earth. The spring was nearly dry at this time of year. Then, in spite of himself, he felt a shudder of fear. There on the ground was the clear impression of a great cat's paw— and another and another. A mountain lion. This huge cat must have been the rabbit's killer. The big tawny marauder had doubtless come here for a drink after his meal of fresh rabbit flesh. Jay knew perfectly well that a lion would not attack him, even if it was lurking nearby. The big cats never did bother people unless they were cornered in a fight, or starving. Still the presence of the killer made an uncontrollable shiver run up his spine. At any rate, there were no sheep tracks. Jay hurried on with his news to the rendezvous at the salt lick above timberline.

"Boy, am I glad we didn't bring the horses along!" Doc said when he heard about the lion. "I wouldn't like to leave them hobbled and helpless anywhere in the timber while we're off hunting. There's nothing that a big cat likes better than horseflesh."

"Well, anyway," Jay said, "it's almost certain the sheep aren't down there among the trees." They all agreed that the sheep would stay away from the lion's hunting area. The boys could continue their search for the bighorns just where they wanted to—high up on the open tundra or on the jagged ridges of the Continental Divide.

The scramble had been strenuous for all of them. They leaned resting their packs against a big boulder at the foot of a semicircular wall of broken, jagged rock. Everywhere around were signs that sheep had bedded down there near the block of salt which had been worn away by their licking tongues.

"Why do you suppose anybody would move a big heavy thing like a block of salt and lug it over to the other side of the ridge?" Jay said wonderingly.

"What do you mean?" Ken asked.

Jay told him the story of what had happened during the summer—how someone had taken the salt and had carried it to the same spot where the sheep had bedded down the year before—how Van's assistants had been nearly killed in a rock slide when they came up to bring the salt to this spot again.

"I still think it was that crazy man with the box," Doc said. "Nothing seems to have been jinxed around here since he cleared out."

"Are you still talking about a 'jinx'?" Ken said, almost irritably. "There's no such thing as a jinx here or anywhere else, and there never has been."

"Then you tell us the reason for all the nutty things that happened last summer," Doc said.

"Let's don't get off on that," Ken said with a smile. "We came after sheep. Let's *go!*"

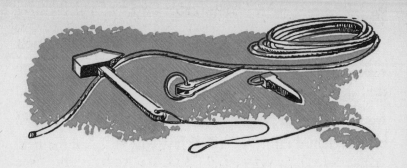

## CHAPTER 17 ... In the Crevasse

By late afternoon, the boys and Ken had swung around the head of the canyon where the Middle Fork of Payrock Creek ran. Moving in a general northerly direction, they kept close under the Continental Divide—sometimes even up on the sharp knife-edge ridge it made at this point. They still had seen no sheep.

Often Jay had stopped and searched along the gray rock masses with the binoculars, but no moving thing appeared except here and there a lumbering marmot or a small cony dashing toward the entrance of its underground home. Then just as the three of them decided it was time to make camp for the night, a chill clear beam of afternoon light fell on a promontory ahead. And there against the horizon stood a mountain sheep.

In a tense whisper, Jay said, "Look! There's one."

Although the strong wind whipped and whistled between the notches in the rocks around them, Doc, too, used the unnecessary precaution of whispering. Even a shout would have been swept away into the depths of the canyon below. "Is it a ram?" he asked Jay, who still had the field glasses. "Look at the horns."

"I know," Jay answered. "No, it's a ewe. There must be more, probably just over the rocks out of sight. Maybe there are rams close by. Let's go."

"Hold on," Ken said. "Look where the sun is. You've got to use your head. It would be dark by the time we climbed to where that sheep is now. Even if the band waited for us, you wouldn't be able to see enough to shoot. In fact, we just about have time enough to find a sheltered place where we can camp for the night. I bet those sheep have been watching us for hours and we didn't know it. If we camp right here near the ridge, they aren't likely to come back past us during the night. Then in the morning when we're fresh we can go after them again."

At first both boys were almost angry that they couldn't go on. Then Jay saw that Ken was talking sense. "I guess you're right," he said. "It's so darn cold already we better find a good spot out of the wind."

"It'll be twice as cold as last night. We're over eleven thousand feet above sea level," said Ken.

Suddenly realizing that he was chilled, Jay swung his arms across his body. An instant later the ewe on the horizon leaped across a chimney in the rock. In three more bounds she was out of sight. Only then did Jay see that she had not been alone on this side of the ridge. The broken shelves and ledges below the skyline seemed alive with leaping figures. Ten or a dozen sheep rose up like springs uncoiling effortlessly. Then they were gone.

"I'm beginning to see why Van said we have to use binoculars," Doc remarked. "Those sheep must have powerful eyes. They can see us move long before we can see them. When we move, they run. That's what happened the day we were on the roundup, Jay. As long as we sat still, they weren't scared. But the minute we moved, they beat it."

Hiking down among the trees, the three of them were soon out of the cutting blasts of wind. They found a flat spot of grass snugly protected on three sides by a thick mass of spruce. Here they threw down their bedrolls and built a small fire.

Next morning, as soon as it grew light enough to see, they were back on the trail. No warming fire now, although it was well below freezing. They were in too great a hurry to get back on the heights where they had seen the bighorns. Sooner than they had expected, the band of sheep appeared in the binoculars, not far from the place where they had left them the night before.

Then began a strange chase along the very backbone of the continent. The forms of the sheep seemed almost like autumn leaves that lifted and leaped on ahead of them, blown by gusts of easy wind. Struggling slowly, heavily, Jay and Doc and Ken heaved each other up over rocky places, inched along knife-edge ridges, and wondered if they would ever get in range. Finally, they lost all sight of the bounding band of sheep. It was long past noon, and they had been so intent on the chase that they hadn't stopped even to munch on the chocolate, raisins, and cheese they had brought for lunch.

By a kind of unspoken agreement, they sank down to rest at last—out of the wind, just above the huge, dirty-gray bulk of Elizabeth Glacier. As Jay bit into his cold, dry food, he found himself looking in wonder at Doc. This cowpoke who hated to hike was doing all right—more than all right. The hunt must mean a lot to him. He had never once asked for a "blow."

Now Doc was on his feet before the other two, restlessly wanting to drive on. "It looks to me," he said, "as if we'll never catch up with those sheep unless we take a short cut. And there it is." He pointed at the mass of glacier ice that filled the canyon between them and the next ragged ridge of rocks.

With the appraising eye of an expert, Ken studied the surface of the glacier. The ice seemed almost flat along its bulging top. He knew there would be chips of rock and gravel and dirt on the surface of the exposed ice. It wouldn't be too difficult to walk there, and it would certainly save them a good hour of slow, tedious scrambling over the chaotic rock ridge at the head of the glacier. Long dark gashes in the ice showed clearly where crevasses had formed as the glacier slipped ponderously down over ledges hidden deep below. But at this time of year, there were no treacherous snow bridges that might cave in and drop them down into the icy depths.

From the glacier, Ken turned methodically to inspect the boots of his companions. Both boys had the heavy composition cleats on their soles that are best for work on slippery surfaces.

"Okay," Ken said. "Let's try it. Just to be on the safe

side, we'll use a rope going across the ice."

"If those sheep are anywhere close by, they'll see us out on the ice. But they might be grazing on the tundra just beyond the far ridge. Then we could sure enough surprise them," Doc said.

They had all been resting in the shelter of a huge boulder. Ken began to take the rope from his pack board. Doc restlessly moved down along the ridge that led to the steep snowbank that fed into the glacier. Jay followed a few paces behind.

"Let me have the field glasses," Doc said to Jay.

"Don't go out on the snow till I get down there with the rope," Ken shouted after them.

With the glasses in hand, Doc moved to the point where the rock ridge ended. From there he would get a clear view of most of the boulders and sharp pinnacles far above. He put the glasses to his eyes and began a search, intently, systematically. He could pick out nothing at all that looked like a sheep. But from where he stood, there was one part of the ridge blocked from view. Forgetting Ken's warning, Doc stepped out a few paces on the heavy, crystalline snow for a better look. Now he could see all of the high sunny ledge that stood out above and beyond him.

Suddenly he called back to Jay in a low tense voice, "Don't move." Then he lowered the glasses slowly to his chest, letting them hang from the leather strap around his neck. With motions as slow as he could make them, he let his gun slip off his shoulder and down his arm, and then he raised it slowly to take aim.

He had sighted an old ram, dozing in the sunlight on that high ledge of rock.

Jay stood as still as one of the boulders around him and watched in feverish fascination. The gun was up now, pointing. Doc shifted his feet ever so slightly to get the best stance, as he kept his eye glued to the telescopic sight. Jay held his breath. Doc was having trouble with his right foot. It seemed to be pressing against an ice ridge in the snow, so that he couldn't place it where he wanted it. Lifting the foot, Doc felt slowly for another spot. Then, as he put it down and rested his full weight on it, something happened.

The snow slithered away.

In a flash, Doc skidded downward. He dropped out of sight in the yawning gap between the snowbank and the edge of the glacier itself!

"Ken!" Jay yelled. "Help! Doc's gone!"

The faint, muffled sound of a cry from Doc rose out of the depths. Ken came scrambling around the big boulder with his coil of rope in one hand and his ice ax in the other. "What happened?" he demanded.

Jay pointed. "Doc was just about to shoot, but his feet slipped. He's down in there."

Ken leaned forward and called, "Doc! Are you hurt?"

A thoroughly frightened voice replied from below, but they couldn't make out the words.

"Anyway, he can yell," Ken said reassuringly to Jay. "You get my pack quick, but be careful."

When Jay returned, Ken had one end of the rope tied around his waist. Quickly he reached into his pack and took out the steel-spiked crampons. He lashed them onto the soles of his boots.

"Jay, you sit here," he said, pointing to a spot where Jay's feet could brace out in front of him against a solid boulder. "Pass this end of the rope around your waist and pay it out gradually to me as I go out on the ice. You can hold me easily if I should fall. I want to see how Doc is fixed, then we'll decide what to do."

Walking slowly, and making sure his crampons bit firmly into the ice at each step, Ken moved out onto the

solid ice of the glacier. Doc's shouts were still muffled, the way noises always are when they come from a deep hole. Opposite the spot from where Doc had slipped, Ken braced himself with one foot behind the other and leaned cautiously over the edge of the chasm.

"Here I am, Doc," he called down. "Don't try to move, yet."

There, twenty feet below Ken, the gap between the glacier and the snowbank narrowed to the point of a kind of V. Wedged in the V between hard snow and harder ice, Doc stood upright.

"Are you all right?" Ken called.

"I don't know," Doc called back. "I'm scared to move. I might slip down farther."

Ken saw that Doc was standing on a lump of snow that had fallen into the crevasse. It wasn't safe for him to try to crawl up the wall of the snowbank, which was almost as hard as ice. Even if there were footholds and handholds, the stuff might give way and send him deeper into the chasm. It would be impossible for him to scale the glistening ice of the glacier itself.

"Stay still," Ken called. "I'll have a rope down to you in a minute."

Using his piton hammer, Ken drove his ice ax into a small crack in the surface of the glacier, well back from the edge of the crevasse. Then he turned to Jay. "Tie the end of the rope around you," he said, "and come on out here. The rope will hold you if you slip."

Now Ken made a turn of the rope around the ice ax and pulled the rope in toward him as Jay approached. When Jay was five paces away from him, Ken ordered, "Now I want you to get behind me a few feet."

Next Ken took out his pocket knife and cut the rope into two lengths. Soon Doc, down in the crevasse, and the two others up on the glacier were all linked together, and all linked to the rope around the ice ax. If any one of them should slip, the ax anchor and the other two could prevent an accident. Now, with Ken hauling on one rope and Doc hoisting his weight up, hand-over-hand on the other rope, they soon had him out.

Without a word, Ken pulled his ice ax out of the glacier and led the other two back to the safety of solid rock.

Pale and shaken, Doc lay down on his back and stared blankly at heavy, gray clouds that had begun to boil up over the peaks above him.

Jay could think of nothing to say except to repeat every

once in a while, "You all right, Doc?" Doc merely nodded his head. Ken looked half relieved and half angry in his silence. Jay could see that Ken was full of a lecture he wanted to give about following a leader's instructions. But he saw also that Ken thought this wasn't just the time to give a speech.

For a long time, while Doc's strength returned, no one said anything. Then, with a start, Jay blurted out, "Hey! the rifle! We got to get it."

"We got to do no such thing!" Ken answered, between tight lips. "The gun's way down the crevasse where it's too narrow to go. We'd have to fish for it maybe for hours. It's too late now. Look at those clouds. It's almost sure to snow. We've got to start home now."

"We'll never get the gun, then," Jay groaned. "Jinxed again."

"That's just too bad," Ken said sarcastically. "Somebody will pick it up a hundred years from now when the glacier has carried it all the way down the canyon."

"But it's not mine!" Doc burst out in distress.

"Well," Ken said, "maybe if it doesn't snow too hard we can come up and try to fish it out next week end. But it's a lot better to go home without a gun than to go back without you. Next time I'll bet you pay attention to some of the simple rules of safety in the mountains."

"I had a perfect shot at that old ram, and I missed my chance," Doc groaned. "I'll probably never get another."

Ken relaxed for the first time and gave Doc a reassuring grin. "I wouldn't feel too bad about everything," he said. "You and Jay did exactly what Van wanted you to do."

Doc sat up. "Are you crazy?" he said.

"Of course, Van didn't want you to lose the gun," Ken answered. "But he didn't really care whether you or any other hunter shot a ram. He didn't tell you why an open season was declared, did he?"

"He certainly did," Doc said. "He said it was to help stop the lung-worm disease."

"Well, that's just what you did," Ken said.

"What do you mean?" Jay asked.

"It's like this," Ken answered. "The fellows in the Game and Fish Department want to get a lot of free work out of hunters. The best way to cure the lung-worm disease is to scatter the sheep and chase them far away from places where they have been bedding down and grazing and catching the sickness. Of course, Van and the other Game and Fish men could have chased the sheep themselves, but it saves them a lot of work if hunters do the job for them."

"Hey, it's a plot!" Jay said, laughing.

"Van said the herds of sheep can spare a few old rams," Ken went on. "In fact, Van's betting there will be more lambs next year than ever. We'll tell him where we've driven the sheep to, and he'll put out new salt to hold them there. Come on. The storm is blowing up in a hurry. Let's get out of here."

"That Van is sure one smart guy," Jay chuckled. "No ordinary brain could get all that hiking out of Doc."

"Well, doggone!" Doc exclaimed. "I don't feel so bad now about losing his gun." But he grinned as he said it.

## CHAPTER 18 ... The Runaway Casualty

Ever since the bighorn hunt, the snow had been piling up, as storms came every few days to the mountains around Payrock. Today—Thanksgiving—a holiday—was perfect for skiing. But Jay felt very little holiday spirit although the store was filled with the smell of roast turkey and of the sage and onions that Grandma Himrod put into the dressing. At noon Jay had stuffed himself on holiday food, but it hadn't been like a real Thanksgiving. He couldn't go skiing. The tantalizing sight of his skis standing upright in the snow outside the store window made him feel even worse.

First, he had to finish loading Grandma's almost empty shelves with new supplies of canned goods. Then he had to spend the rest of the day, and probably a lot of the night, reading a book. When school began, his English teacher had assigned *Ivanhoe* as outside reading. Jay had intended to read it, but something had always come up. Usually the something was a class in the Rescue Squad climbing school.

The trouble was, his teacher was just too smart. She had figured out that some kids might try to fool her by seeing the movie of *Ivanhoe* instead of reading the book itself. In desperation, that was what Jay had done. And the examination proved it. The teacher asked questions on the final test that you could only answer correctly if you had read the book—every word of it. The result showed up on his report card. Now Grandma had forbidden any skiing until he had made up his back work so he could take the examination over. This wouldn't have been so bad, except for the fact that he had special plans for tomorrow.

Tomorrow Ken Schultz would bring Doc and three of the Rescue Squad members to spend the holiday skiing around Payrock. The whole thing had been planned out so well. Ken was going to stay with Jay at the store. Doc had permission to open his family's ranch house up on the hill. The other Squad members would sleep there as his guests. Grandma would give them all a big leftover turkey dinner tomorrow, after a day of practice on the nearby ski

slopes. But Jay might have to stay in all day tomorrow—
if he didn't get that darned book read.

He glanced at Grandma rocking comfortably beside the
potbellied stove in the middle of the store. She was dozing
from the big Thanksgiving dinner and the heat of the stove.
But Jay knew that if he opened the door and tried to
step out for even one quick run on his skis, she would be
wide awake. She was just too smart, like his teacher. Jay
hadn't brought *Ivanhoe* with him for the holiday. But
when Grandma saw the bad mark on his report card, she
unlocked her glass-covered bookcase and took out the copy
of the book that his father had used in school. Jay had
read it in bed last night until he had fallen asleep. In a few
minutes he would have to go back to it again—unless
maybe Grandma began to snore in deep sleep.

As quietly as he could, Jay arranged the cans on the
shelves. Then suddenly a rattle shattered his plans for
temporary escape. Benzy was up to something in the rooms
behind the store. In a moment the little dog began to paw
and scratch at the other side of the swinging door. Then
he shoved it open and backed along the floor, pulling
something heavy. When his small yellow form emerged
from behind the counter at the rear of the store, Grandma

was awake. Both she and Jay saw at the same moment the latest item in Benzy's long list of stolen goods.

Grandma, for once, didn't scold. Instead she laughed quietly to herself.

"Good dog!" she said, patting the surprised animal with genuine approval. "That's the first time you ever did a useful thing in your life." Then, to Jay, "Here, Benzy's brought you 'Ivanhoe.' You can quit work on those shelves now and do some reading. Wasn't that nice of him?" she added, mischievously.

With a kind of hopeless feeling that the whole world was against him, Jay picked up the battered old volume and went back to his room. The worst of it was Grandma knew the book as well as the teacher did. She was sure to quiz him on it before she let him go skiing tomorrow.

When Grandma called him for supper, Jay was surprised at how far he had got into the story and how much he really wanted to finish it. He was all primed to answer any quiz she gave him. But again she fooled him. She wanted to know about the climbing school!

It had never occurred to Grandma that there was anything to learn about climbing mountains. You just went out and did it, she thought. She had been all over the hills

herself when she was young, wearing the long skirts that every proper young lady wore, even in the wilderness.

So, as Jay ate turkey giblets, he told her about the afternoon classes that the Rescue Squad held on the sandstone rocks in the foothills near Fremont College campus. With an old piece of clothesline, he demonstrated knots and showed how he could rappel down the wall of the dining room—if only the ceiling weren't there. He stuck a can opener in a crack in the wall to show her how pitons were used. He called out some of the signals that Ken had taught him: "On belay!" "Off belay!"

Through all this, Benzy sat still as long as he could. Then he began tugging at the clothesline Jay had tied around himself to demonstrate a safety rope. That reminded Grandma.

"I guess I've had enough climbing lessons for tonight," she said. "Now you go back to 'Ivanhoe.' I'll do the dishes."

This time Jay didn't mind too much returning to his homework, and he read on and on until the job was done. Next morning he slept late—so late, in fact, that the first thing he heard was a raucous honking of automobile horns in front of the store. Ken and Doc and the others were already here, he realized in dismay, and they all kidded him unmercifully when he came out in his bathrobe to greet them.

As if nothing had happened, Grandma announced, "Hurry up, Jay, I've got hot breakfast for everybody. You fellows come into the kitchen, but don't you try any of your climbing stunts the way this mountain goat was showing me last night."

After breakfast all six of them trooped out in front of the store to wax their skis, test their ski harness, slap the long thin boards resoundingly on the hard-packed snow of the road, and practice glide steps like skaters. They had to wait a while for Doc who was slower than the others. Doc had only been on skis a few times in his life. He was clumsy at adjusting his harness and clumsier when he tried to keep his balance on the slick road.

Soon they were all out on top of the open slope that descended into the almost-deserted town. One after another they streaked down the hill, making graceful Christiania swings as they broke the pure surface of the snow. All of them, that is, except Doc. He tangled up half a dozen times before he got halfway down.

"You're trying too hard," Ken told him in a friendly way. "Just snowplow, or stem, at first—like this." Then he demonstrated what complete control this pigeon-toed way of skiing, called snowplowing, could give. It still seemed a miracle to Doc that the long clumsy boards fastened to his feet could ever be made into delicate tools that he could control with great precision.

Jay marveled, too. Here was Ken, full-grown, but not as tall as he was, squarish-built and almost lumpy—but suddenly Ken could swoop down the hill with all the grace and perfection of a bird in flight. Time and again Jay himself sped along the slope, practicing turns as he went and making quick stops at the bottom.

When he curved and swept down the hill, something inside him seemed almost ready to explode with the sense of excitement and power that the well-executed ski run gave him. At the bottom, he looked back up the slope at the slender, winding trace he had left in the snow. Nothing in the world, he thought, was more satisfying than skiing, not even hiking to the top of the highest, hardest peak.

The day seemed only well begun when Grandma stepped out of the store and jangled an old cow bell. It was hard to believe that lunch time had come already. Each skier completed one more triumphant glide—even Doc, who ended up with something of a flourish in front of the store.

That afternoon the wild, free independence of the morning practice was over. Ken had planned some drills to prepare them for wintertime rescue work.

"Somebody's got to be the casualty," Ken announced.

"That's me," Doc said, beaming. "The book says I've got two hundred and twelve bones. Most of 'em feel broken right now."

"Okay," Ken laughed. "You're going to get some free rides down the hill."

"How about up?" Doc asked, looking pained. "Don't you have to practice bringing casualties uphill?"

The others, fearing that Doc had Ken in a trap, began to protest loudly. "Did you ever hear of a rescue that went *up* a mountain?" one of them asked. "These mountains all run downhill."

"I'll tell you what," Jay said. "We'll split the difference. I'll be the casualty half the time—the uphill half."

Ken just grinned and said, "Come on, let's get ready."

At the top of the slope, Ken told Doc to take off his skis. Next he lashed the two skis together, making them into a sort of toboggan. Then he and two of the others took off their outer jackets to make a padding on top of the skis. They would be warm enough as long as they kept active.

"Now," Ken said, "you've got a broken leg, Doc."

"Broken back, too," Doc said with enthusiasm.

"Lie down in the snow," Ken directed.

Doc jubilantly flopped backward, sending a shower of powdery snow over the bystanders. "Help! Help!" he cried and thrashed his arms around to make sure everybody got a dose of snow.

"Tell him he's unconscious, Ken," Jay yelled.

"You're out cold," said Ken.

"I sure am cold," Doc responded. "Snow down my neck. Hurry up and rescue me."

The Squad members took Doc's ski poles and two more jackets and fashioned them into an emergency splint on Doc's "broken" leg. Then, working two on each side, they lifted him onto the toboggan as carefully as if they were handling eggs.

"No fair tickling," Doc warned them.

Now, as Doc lay with his feet toward the upturned points of the skis, Ken took a light nylon cord and tied Doc securely to the toboggan. Next he fastened a heavier rope under Doc's armpits. "Jay, you hang onto the rope," he said. "I'm going to straddle Doc and guide this ski-toboggan down the hill. You, Jay, will come along behind,

holding the safety rope to act as a brake in case the toboggan gets away from me."

"You mean I've got to run along behind on foot?" Jay
asked. "The snow's too deep for that."

"No, we'll both ski," Ken said. "You just snowplow all
the way down. Hold the rope with one hand. Take both
your ski poles in the other. I'll tuck my poles in along Doc's
tummy here. We'll need the poles coming back up."

While the final preparations were being made, Doc had
become suddenly very quiet. Jay wondered if he was scared,
but he didn't have long to wonder, for they were soon off
on a slow, controlled slide down the hill.

Ken had to ski bent almost double, holding the tips of
the toboggan skis in his hands to steady them. His own
skis were spread wide apart, one on either side of Doc. Ken
kept his skis toed-in, so that at first Jay had little to worry
about in his job as brakeman.

Then all at once, Doc let out a realistic yell as if he
were in mortal pain from his injuries. "Oh, my aching
back!" he cried.

Ken was so startled that he turned involuntarily to see
what had happened. His pigeon-toed skis crossed each
other, and the next thing anybody knew he had sailed

through the air and piled up headfirst in the snow.

The screaming patient on the ski toboggan zoomed past him, picking up speed before Jay had presence of mind enough to brake it. Jay saw Doc wave derisively at Ken's tangled legs sticking out of the snow. The patient was in good shape, mighty good shape!

On impulse, Jay dropped the rope. If Doc wanted some fun on this ride, let him have some real fun. But the instant he let the rope go, he felt a surge of alarm. Too late he realized Doc couldn't guide the toboggan, and he couldn't get off. In the town below there were buildings he might crash into.

Maybe, Jay thought, he could catch up with Doc in time. Urging himself downhill with his poles, he glided in a racing crouch. But there was no overtaking the toboggan. Behind the first building snow had drifted, and the speeding toboggan swerved out of danger when it met the drift. Another drift guided it away from the next building—then straight out onto the icy, glistening surface of the road. On went the skis with their helpless bundle.

Doc was still yelling, but now the cries for help were real and from the heart. He passed the store and sailed on between the two high banks left on either side of the road

by the snow plow. Beyond the store the road dipped sharply into the canyon. Gathering more and more speed, the toboggan slithered on down the road.

Before Doc reached the flat place at the bottom of the half-mile stretch of road, the other skiers caught up with Jay who stood transfixed, helplessly watching his friend careen down the canyon. With his face white from terror, Jay kept muttering, "If a car comes—if a car comes—"

Doc could not possibly avoid smashing into a car or truck if one should be coming up the road. At last Doc disappeared around a bend and was out of sight. The rest of them glided off at top speed after him. The icy surface of the road made skiing tricky work. If they had been in no hurry, any one in the party could have made the slide without a tumble. But in the excitement all of them fell at least once, and Jay went down several times. He was the last to reach the flats.

There, way off the road, he saw Doc clambering out of the elaborate rigging that had held him to the ski-toboggan. He had ridden right up over the side of the snowbank on the last turn and had landed in a perfect cushion of a drift.

A great smile of delight filled Doc's round face as the

others pushed their skis through the soft snow toward him. He seemed completely over his first fear. The excitement of the ride was uppermost in his mind, now.

One after another the skiers asked, "Are you all right?" They crowded anxiously around him.

"Who's going to pull me back up?" Doc answered, paying no attention to the questions.

"Nobody!" Ken snapped in anger. He was angry at himself for letting Doc startle him into a spill, but he was mad at Doc, too, for having played the trick on him.

Jay hung behind a little. He hadn't crowded as close to Doc as the others. He stared at their backs and wondered. Should he confess to Ken that he had let go the rope and started Doc on his wild and dangerous slide, just for the heck of it?

## CHAPTER 19 ... Reward Offered

After the dishes were washed that evening, Doc led three of the college boys up the hill to the Martins' ranch house where they would spend the night. Now Grandma sat in her usual place, the rocking chair by the pot-bellied stove in the center of the store. Ken and Jay, on straight-backed chairs, toasted their stockinged feet in the heat the old stove gave off.

The words of Ken's angry lecture on safety—and against pranks in the mountains—were still tumbling around in Jay's mind. Jay hadn't confessed that he let the toboggan rope go on purpose. Every minute that passed made it harder to tell. And every minute was acute torture. Jay felt sure the Rescue Squad would *never* make him a member if they knew that he had endangered his best friend's life by a foolish stunt.

"You look plumb tuckered out, Jay," Grandma observed, finally. "You better go to bed."

"Guess you're right," Jay answered in a meek voice. He lifted Benzy off his lap where the little yellow dog had been sleeping peacefully. But before he reached the swinging door at the back of the store, the phone rang. He padded over to answer it. In a moment he turned.

"It's for you, Ken. It's the sheriff! Do you suppose we have to go out on a rescue tonight?"

All Jay could hear of the conversation was Ken's, "Yes . . . no . . . uh-huh. . . . Tomorrow and the next day, then . . . . All right . . . okay. We'll do it."

Suddenly Jay's silence and sleepiness were gone. "What's up?" he asked eagerly as Ken turned away from the phone. "Somebody hurt or lost or what?"

Ken in his deliberate way settled down by the stove again before he responded to Jay's questions. "That was Sheriff McKenney," he said. "He's got a job for us tomorrow."

"Not tonight?" Jay asked, almost disappointed. He had visions of taking a long, hazardous trip in the moonlight to save the life of some stranded skier.

"No rush," Ken replied. "Here's the story. You remember that uranium prospector?"

"You mean the man with the box!" Jay exclaimed. "The jinxer!"

Ken smiled tolerantly. "Well, the man with the Geiger counter, let's call him. The sheriff said he just received a circular about the fellow. It was sent up from Texas."

"Like those 'Criminals Wanted' things in the post office?"

"Something like that, I guess."

"I bet he escaped from a loony asylum and they're trying to find him," said Jay. "We told you he was crazy."

"For land's sakes, let Ken tell his story," Grandma broke in.

"There's nothing in the circular about his being crazy or a criminal," Ken said patiently. "His friend, the man who owns Camp Wapiti, is offering a five-hundred-dollar reward to anybody who provides information leading to the discovery of his whereabouts. The circular says he was last seen heading up toward the Divide from Camp Wapiti. I guess I must have been almost the last person to see him, come to think of it. Anyway, the fellow never showed up to collect his mail in Humboldt. He didn't go back to Texas, either. The sheriff thinks he may be living in some old shack around here, the same way he lived in that

Doubtful Mine shack last summer."

"He sure hasn't come in here for food or supplies," Grandma said. "I haven't seen any strangers since the end of the tourist season."

"He might have cached enough stuff that he got from Wapiti to last him the whole winter, although I doubt it," Ken said. "Anyway, the sheriff wants us to have a look-see at all the old cabins we can visit in two days."

"All I have to say," Grandma put in, "is that anybody who stays alone in these mountains is either crazy or dead. Unless it's an old-timer like me and Ashy—and sometimes I think we ought to know better," she added with a chuckle.

"If he's dead, there's no use looking for him," Jay said.

"No, you're wrong," Ken said. "His friends want to know exactly what has happened to him. If we find out, we'll get a good reward, and the Squad can sure use the money for equipment."

"You mean you go looking for people that have been dead a long time?" Jay asked in amazement.

"Once in a while we have to," Ken answered grimly. "We had to a couple of years ago. Some people just won't believe us when we tell them they ought to leave word about where they are going and when they expect to come back. The body we located could have belonged to a live man if he had just left word about his plans. By the time we found him it was too late. And it wasn't our fault."

"Excuse me a minute," Jay said. While Grandma and Ken kept on talking, Jay went quietly to his room. In another moment he was grinding hard on the crank of the private telephone between his room and Doc's house.

Urgently he told Doc the news about the man with the box. Doc said he would bring the gang down right away to hear about it. "Wait, don't hang up," Jay said. Then he hesitated, fumbling for words. "There—there's something I want to tell you, and I'm sorry, but don't tell anybody else, please. I thought it was just a joke and didn't realize what I'd done. I let go of that rope this afternoon on purpose. I'm going to tell Ken somehow that I'm as much to blame as you are, but please let me do it. Don't you dare do it. Now hurry on down here."

"Well, doggone, anyway!" Doc exclaimed. "Say, are we going to work telepathy on Ken?"

"Good idea," Jay said. "He doesn't know I called you. Hurry up."

Jay took time enough in the kitchen at the back of the house to eat a chunk of pie. He had been so worried at

suppertime that he had lost his appetite. Now a great weight was off his mind. He had confessed to Doc, at least. Even though he still had the job of telling Ken sometime, he could enjoy pie again.

Almost at the instant Jay re-entered the store, there came a swish and slap of skis on the road outside, then a series of thunderous poundings of ski boots on the platform in front of the door. Doc burst in ahead of the others, his round cheeks pink from the frosty air.

"When do we start looking for the man with the box?" he demanded abruptly.

"Yeah, Ken, why didn't you tell us at suppertime?" one of the Squad members demanded.

Ken looked mystified. "I just got a call," he said. "Only about five minutes ago. But how did you find out?"

"Doc told us. We were going to bed, but Doc said we had to hurry on down here for a conference."

"Did the sheriff call you, Doc?" Ken asked.

"He couldn't have," Grandma said innocently. "Doc's phone was disconnected when his folks moved down to Fremont last fall."

Ken looked cautiously from Doc to Jay and back again. Together the boys almost chanted, "It's telepathy—

mountain telepathy. We got it."

"And tomorrow," Jay added, "I'm going to find that jinxer or know the reason why."

Something told Ken he had better not pursue the telepathy angle too far right now. Instead, he switched in businesslike fashion to the problems of the search. "Don't think for a minute we're likely to find anything tomorrow or next day," he said. Then he turned to the other Squad members. "The sheriff heard we were up here, and he thought we might like to do something useful while we're practicing."

Ken reviewed all the known facts about the man with the box. Then he said, "It seems to me there are three possibilities. One—the fellow is living in an abandoned cabin somewhere back of here. Two—he's died somewhere, probably in the Devil's Crater area. Three—he's just disappeared for reasons of his own and is alive some place without letting his friends know it. We'll be able to take care of number one this week end. If we don't find him alive, we'll wait till spring and look into number two as early in the spring as we can get into Devil's Crater. Then if we don't find a body, I guess the reward will be out of the question, at least as far as we're concerned. Five hundred dollars would sure get us some good equipment."

"I'm surprised to hear that you do your rescue work for money," Grandma said, a little tartly.

"Oh, no, of course we don't," Ken answered, looking almost hurt. "We never charge anything. That's the trouble. It costs us a lot of our own personal money. The equipment is expensive, and there are things we need right now that we can't pay for. If this man's friends think it is worth five hundred dollars to find out what's happened to him, I guess we're doing a good thing by trying to help, aren't we?"

"I see," Grandma said. "But I can tell you one thing. You won't find out anything tomorrow."

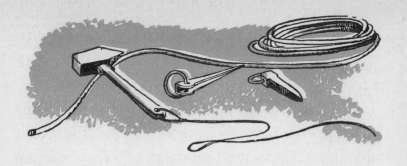

## CHAPTER 20 ... Into Devil's Crater

Grandma Himrod was right. Every trace of the man with the box had disappeared. The searchers found absolutely no signs of him in their two days of cross-country skiing.

After that, all winter long Jay and Doc talked about him and the jinx. They agreed on one thing. Ever since the man disappeared there had been no new reports of freak accidents and strange goings-on in Payrock Canyon. Talk about troubles in the Canyon had died down. The jinx seemed to have frozen up with the coming of winter.

"Of course, you got to admit," Doc said, "with four feet of snow on the level, people aren't going much farther than Grandma's store. So there's not much chance for a jinx to operate. Something might happen to Ashy, of course, but he's always been there, and he knows how to take care of himself."

"Just the same," Jay said, "I wouldn't like to see trouble start again next summer."

"Me neither," Doc said with real feeling. "I have to look after our cattle, and I like it peaceful up there the way it used to be."

"I'm just positive," Jay said, "if we find the man with the box, dead or alive, we'll have the clue to everything."

The Rescue Squad was as much interested in the uranium prospector as Jay was, but for a different reason. Weeks before the snow was off the ground, the Squad members began making plans for a foot-by-foot search of the entire Devil's Crater region. Several times Jay sat in on the planning sessions. He joined Ken and the others in poring over maps of the wilderness area. He listened as they made up lists of the equipment they would need: coils of new nylon rope for each member, a lot of new pitons, new batteries for the walkie-talkies, new, highly condensed rations they wanted to experiment with. Things that seemed strange to Jay turned up on the lists, too—drawing paper, pencils, cameras.

Ken explained what these items were for. It might take many week ends of intensive search to locate the man's body —if, indeed, it was there. The search had to include every inch of the giant, jagged collar of rock that surrounded Devil's Crater. The Squad members would take photographs from various angles all around the Crater. Then they would enlarge these and study them. The enlargements would show where a man who was prospecting might think he could climb. The drawing paper and pencils were for detailed sketches of chimneys, chutes, ledges. These sketches and photographs would be used in planning a systematic combing of the area.

All this fascinated Jay, but it also made him impatient. "I'm sick of all this talk, talk, talk," he said to Doc one night after a long meeting. "They'd have just as much luck if they simply started out hiking and looked, when the snow is off the ground. They'll still be making plans the middle of next summer, and by that time the jinx may be jinxing again."

"Let 'em plan," was Doc's reply. "But you better get your homework done, or Grandma won't let you go on any of their trips to the Crater."

"Don't you want to come, too?" Jay asked.

"I guess I wouldn't mind making one trip," Doc answered. "I've never been down in Devil's Crater and it might be fun to see all these scientific sleuths use their gadgets. But I'd still rather ride Buck any day than sniff around the mountains for the carcass of a man that was crazy in the first place."

As spring came to the plains, the date for the first search trip was set—the long Decoration Day week end. Suddenly Jay began to feel uneasy. All winter he had assumed he would be invited to go. He had not missed a climbing school session yet, and Ken had casually asked him several times if he wanted to attend meetings to plan the search. But now, Jay realized, Ken had never actually asked him to go along.

One thing particularly worried Jay. He had never found exactly the right chance to confess that he turned Doc loose on the ski-toboggan at Thanksgiving time. His guilty conscience made him wonder if Ken somehow knew this. Ken was so serious about safety in the mountains that he might make Jay miss the Devil's Crater trip in order to teach him a lesson.

And so, Jay was greatly relieved when Ken said in an offhand way one night late in May, "Jay, do you think your grandmother will let you off next week end so we can make our first reconnaissance trip?"

"You mean I can go with you?" Jay asked.

"Why, sure. That's been part of the plan all along," Ken answered. "You and Doc and I have the most important job to do on the first day. I figured we could get a head start by staying Friday night in Payrock. We'll leave my car at Camp Wapiti and go over into the Crater from this side."

"I thought the search was going to start from the other side of the Divide and work up into the Crater that way," Jay said.

"Yeah, two carloads are going to do that," Ken answered. "But we have to follow the trail from this side. I was probably the last one to see the prospector headed toward the Crater last fall. In this work you can't take anything for granted. We must start from the known fact that he was going into the Crater from this side. If by any chance we should find him quickly, that'll be all there is to it."

Although Grandma Himrod needed Jay, she said he could go. But she made it quite clear that he couldn't expect to have week ends off all summer. Tourists would soon begin to arrive.

And so Saturday morning found Jay, Doc, and Ken starting their first trip into the high back country. It was just after daylight when they came to Lucky Lake.

"Oh, oh," Doc said. "Looks like we're going to have trouble." He pointed ahead where snowdrifts spilled out from under the protecting branches of a thick stand of Engelmann spruce. "Why don't we leave the car here? If we have to shovel through drifts, it will be tough going. We could head up to the Divide from here. And besides, we can stop and see if those beavers have changed from black to brown."

"Don't start that jinx talk again," Ken said. "Beavers don't change color."

"Well, Van said they'd been doing it," Doc answered. "He asked us last year to keep an eye on the preserve."

"You'll have to do it some other time," Ken answered. "The whole point of going into Devil's Crater from this side is to follow the trail that prospector took. It begins over on the South Fork above Ashy's cabin. Hop out, boys. It will be quicker to shovel through the snow and drive on than to walk all the way."

The lingering drifts weren't large, and the car soon reached the beginning of the trail—the trail they had followed on their hunt for the mountain sheep. Their packs were heavier now, for they carried a good deal more mountain-climbing gear than they had in September. As they strode uphill toward Ashy's cabin, Jay and Doc poked occasional fun at Ken. In addition to his heavy pack, Ken carried one of the walkie-talkies, hung at his side from a strap over his shoulder. In voices loud enough so Ken could overhear, they kept talking about "the man with the box," and looking his way. But Ken was a hard guy to tease very satisfactorily. He was so dead serious about everything he did, and somehow he always seemed to be right.

All three of them looked forward to a pause at Ashy's house. Possibly the old man would even give them a cup of hot coffee if he was in a good humor. So they were mildly disappointed when they found the door to his weathered log cabin padlocked. A wisp of smoke from the chimney showed that Ashy hadn't been away long. Not far above the cabin, they found that his tracks led up the trail they were going to follow.

Above timberline, wind had blown the tundra free of snow, except for occasional pockets behind knobs of rock. Underfoot the sod was spongy and full of moisture. The little gray conies sat bolt upright in the sun, whistling warnings to each other as the hikers approached.

"I sure wish we'd brought Benzy," Jay said. "He'd have

the time of his life chasing those conies."

"It's just as well you left him home," Ken said. "We might have a lot of trouble getting him down into the Crater. I'm sure we'll have to use ropes. Besides, we've got waterproof boots on, but a day or two of running around in ice-cold puddles of water wouldn't do Benzy any good."

All during the steady climb from timberline to that great heap of rocks called Granny's Wart on the Continental Divide, the three of them saw signs that Ashy was somewhere ahead of them.

"Sure looks like you have to get up early to be ahead of that old boy," Ken said. "I wonder what he's doing up this way. It doesn't look like good country to hunt for junk in."

"Maybe he heard about the five-hundred-dollar reward and decided to get there first," Jay suggested. "Grandma sure enough might have told him. He hikes his legs off looking for scraps of old iron, and I bet you anything he'd spend the whole summer trying to get the reward. Wouldn't it be just our luck if he beats us to it!"

"It is certainly bad judgment for an old man to hike around alone in this wild country," Ken said. "I don't care how experienced or how tough he is. If anything happened to him, nobody would be likely to miss him until it was too late."

When they reached Granny's Wart, Ken called for a "blow," and while the boys rested he dropped his pack and went on in the direction of Ashy's tracks. They were faint now. Moisture had already drained out of the thin patches of moss here on the roof of the world. But occasionally a footprint showed on protected patches of snow. It was freezing cold in the brilliant sunlight, and the boys were eager to move on.

"I wonder—I wonder," Ken said reflectively as he rejoined them. "The regular trail down into Devil's Crater drops over the Divide right here." He pointed down the western side of the Divide, which was much steeper and more rugged than the rolling tundra they had crossed on the way up. Actually there was no trail visible to the boys, but they could see two small cairns—heaps of stone they knew from experience had been piled there by previous hiking parties to mark the best way down.

"What are you wondering about?" Jay asked.

"A lot of things," Ken answered. "Ashy's tracks don't follow the regular trail. It looks as if he knows another trail into the Crater, one I never heard of. Now, should we follow his tracks, so we can learn a new way into the Crater? Or shall we follow the old trail? There's no telling which way the prospector would have gone. Maybe he didn't see those cairns, and maybe he knew there was another route."

"Let's follow Ashy's tracks," Jay proposed. "We can always follow the cairns, but the tracks won't last."

"That's a good idea," Ken agreed. "We can come back up the regular trail later."

"Let's go," Doc called out, guide fashion.

"No, we have to wait till eleven o'clock. That's only fifteen minutes." Ken said. "If we're going to change our course, I want to notify the fellows who are coming up the valley into the Crater. Possibly, they might even have found the prospector already and want us down there in a hurry."

Ken opened up the walkie-talkie box. He put the receiver to his ear and listened. State Highway Patrol officers were making routine reports on the same wave length as that of his set. By agreement with the Patrol, the Rescue Squad members were allowed to break in at regular intervals and do their talking, while the Patrol gave them uninterrupted use of the air.

"One-oh-five to one-oh-six," Ken said into his mouth-piece on the exact stroke of eleven. "One-oh-five to one-oh-six."

From far below in the black depths of the forest-covered bottom of the Crater came back a voice: "One-oh-six receiving. One-oh-five go ahead."

Ken reported his position and told of discovering a possible new trail. He learned that the main party at the lower end of the Crater had found nothing so far. It was agreed that he and the two boys should try the new route. They would report again in half an hour.

Ken put the receiver back in the carrying case and pushed the telescoping aerial down into the box out of the way. "Okay. It'll be Ashy's route," he said. "Let's go."

The faint trail left by the old man's boots led down toward a chute. At the head of the chute was a steep slope covered with loose rubble. Then a series of giant steps, each one dropping off three or four feet, went straight down between walls of rock that appeared to be almost perpendicular.

"This is easy," Ken said. "So far it's better than the regular trail. But we don't know what's coming, so we'll use a rope."

Ken tied one end of his rope around Jay's waist, passed the middle of the rope around Doc's waist and knotted it. Then he tied the other end around himself.

"Doc, you take up all the slack between you and Jay and keep the extra rope in a coil in your hand," Ken said.

The boys knew what to do now. "Number one, go," Ken called to Jay who was in the lead. Doc paid out the rope that was coiled in his hand, as Jay went down the chute. When Jay reached the end of the rope, he stopped. "Number two, go," Ken said. Doc moved forward as Ken paid out the rope. Then Doc stopped, waiting for Ken to catch up. There were always two of the three of them standing still and well braced, while the third maneuvered down the chute. It was slow but safe.

"It's a wonder someone in the hiking club didn't find this route before," Ken said. "It's a natural. But I can see how people missed it when they came over the Divide the way we did. Granny's Wart is at the low point in the ridge, and they naturally headed for that, and then they just went on down from there. I suppose nobody has really explored the whole Crater. Darn few people ever get in here. Everybody says that the fishing isn't even worth bothering about."

Ken looked at his watch. It was not yet time for his eleven-thirty walkie-talkie call.

A jumble of freshly loosened rock lay just below Jay. He worked toward it and cautiously tested the pile to see if it would hold him without slipping. Then he sat for a moment resting his weight on his hands and heels and the seat of his pants. Suddenly, as he pushed at one loose stone with his boot, he let out an involuntary horrified cry:

"Ashy!"

The stone had rolled away, revealing the battered miner's cap that Ashy always wore. Here was the old man's limp form, crumpled up and pressed so close to a boulder that Jay had not seen him over its bulging top. The loose stones held him and kept him from tumbling downward, and the gnarled shape of a stunted tree that grew out of a rock crevice gave him some support.

"What?" Doc yelled.

"Take it easy!" Ken ordered. "What's up, Jay?"

"Ashy's here, I tell you! He's been knocked out or something by some rocks. What'll I do?" Jay cried.

"Can you get over to solid footing anywhere?" Ken asked.

"I—I guess I can if you two hold tight," Jay answered.

Carefully supporting as much of his weight as he could by his hands on little projections in the rock, Jay eased himself over onto a solid ledge just beyond the place where Ashy was propped up in the midst of the rubble.

"Ken, I think I know what to do," Jay called. "You and Doc stay where you are and pass me down a safety line. I'll tie it around Ashy so he can't roll downhill if any of these rocks should give way while one of you is getting here."

"Right," Ken answered.

In a moment the inert figure of the old man was secured and Ken was standing beside Jay. Carefully they moved rocks and the tangled branches of the small timberline tree. Ashy was alive, but a welt on his head suggested that he had been knocked out by a blow. He must have been caught in one of the countless small rock slides that came with spring thaws.

Gently Ken eased the old man over till he was lying free of the stones and leaning back against his rucksack. Slowly Ashy began to open his eyes. They gazed uncertainly out of a face that was as white as his beard. He seemed trying to recall where he was and what had happened. Then he stirred slightly, groaned, and looked from Jay to Ken

and back again, as if trying to solve some problem in his mind.

"Where are you hurt?" Ken asked.

Ashy just shook his head in silence and breathed deeply, as though that would help shut out pain that was obviously there.

In spite of the excitement, Ken hadn't forgotten to keep one eye on his wrist watch. At exactly eleven-thirty he made his radio call to the main party at the mouth of Devil's Crater. Quickly he reported the accident and said he would call again at twelve when he had found out what shape Ashy was really in. Then they would decide what was the best thing to do.

From now on Ken moved with quiet speed and efficiency. There was no longer need for him and the boys to be roped together. So the three of them made Ashy as comfortable as they could on one of their sleeping bags with another used as a cover. The sun was bright, but the wind blew chill, and Ashy seemed to be suffering from shock. He needed to be kept warm. Up to now he had said nothing.

Then, in his characteristic blunt way, he grumbled, "What you fellows doing over here, anyway?"

Jay smiled and thought to himself, "Ornery old crosspatch. Here we are saving his life and he's crabbing because we're around." Aloud he told Ashy briefly about the search for the man with the box.

Ken, who had been thinking out strategy, broke in now. "Can't you tell us where you're hurt?" he asked.

"My leg," Ashy answered. "I think it's busted. Know it's busted, in fact. What you going to do about it?"

"We'll get you out. Don't you worry about that," Ken answered.

"How did it happen?" Doc asked.

"Who were you talking to on that radio box?" Ashy asked, paying no attention to Doc.

Ken explained about the party of nine searchers who were working their way into the Crater from the northwest. He had made up his mind by now that it would be quicker to take Ashy back over the bare slope toward his own cabin than to carry him out through the miles and miles of heavy timber along the Crater bottom. He explained all this to the old man.

"We'll have a stretcher rigged up for you in no time," Ken finished. "Jay, you come with me. We'll hike down a ways below timberline and get a couple of saplings."

Before time for the next walkie-talkie report, they had

brought back two slender spruce poles. Jay cut holes at the bottom of one of the sleeping bags. Then he and Doc pushed the poles through the bag to make a stretcher. Meanwhile, Ken reported his plan by radio. The nine Squad members far down in the valley were to continue their search. Ken, Jay, and Doc would carry the old man on the improvised stretcher up the short distance to the ridge, then down the easy trail to his cabin. There, Ken would spend the night with Ashy while Jay and Doc went back to Payrock to summon an ambulance.

Clearly something was on Ashy's mind. "Wait a minute," he said as they started to lift him onto the stretcher, after Ken had put an emergency splint on his leg.

"I can save your Rescue Squad some trouble," the old man groaned, then held his breath at a twinge of pain in his leg. "That crazy man left this neck of the woods about a week ago."

"A week ago!" Jay exclaimed. "You mean he's alive?"

"He sure is—and crazier than ever," Ashy answered. "Anybody would have to be double-darned crazy to spend the winter in Devil's Crater hunting for uranium."

"How do you know that he spent the winter down there?" Ken asked.

"I saw him over there a couple of weeks ago—saw the cabin he built down on the crick that runs into Devil's Lake, too."

"Well, I'll be—" Ken exclaimed.

"How do you know he's gone?" Jay asked.

"I watched him packing out down the valley," Ashy answered. "Then I went over to his cabin. He'd sure left it for good. Took everything with him that was worth taking."

"How about that!" Doc said. "All this hike for nothing."

Ashy snorted. "What you mean for nothing? Where would I be if you hadn't come along?"

Doc was embarrassed. "Well, you know what I mean, Ashy."

Ashy turned to Ken. "You better use that radio box of yours and tell the rest of your gang to save their energy. I bet you that prospector is clear back to Texas by now— if they haven't caught him on the way and locked him up in a loony house."

"I can't call now," Ken said, a little shamefaced. "That was dumb of me. They won't start listening for another call from me until noon tomorrow. I told them I'd try to get back within talking distance by then. You see, these machines aren't powerful enough to send and receive when there's a mountain between them."

"Then quit stalling around," Ashy said crossly. "Get me out of here."

## CHAPTER 21 ... Clues to the Unexpected

"Boy, that's a neat gadget," Doc said admiringly. "What's the least you have to do to yourself to rate a ride in it? It's sure a lot better than hiking."

Doc stood with Ken and Jay in front of Ashy's cabin as two ambulance attendants wheeled the old man down the trail in a newfangled kind of litter. The litter was made of lightweight aluminum rods mounted on a bicycle wheel and complete with padding and springs to absorb shocks from the rocky trail.

Jay grinned. "That thing sure would have been a help yesterday when we had to lug Ashy all the way here by hand."

Ken was obviously filled with pride. The Rescue Squad had worked hard to raise money to buy this special litter, which was imported from Austria where it was used in

Alpine rescues. Now it was getting its first practical test. He wished he could go along with the men to see how it negotiated every turn on the way down to the ambulance that was waiting at Camp Wapiti. But he had promised to check in on the walkie-talkie at noon today and give a report to the Squad members down in Devil's Crater.

Suddenly a little yellow form emerged from the woods, took one look at the strange vehicle, and went after it at top speed.

"Here, Benzy, Benzy!" Jay called.

"How did he get here?" Ken asked in surprise.

"Oh, he chased us up the road this morning and wouldn't go home. So we decided to give him a lift in your car," Jay answered.

"We wanted to save his legs from being worn off any shorter than they already are," Doc added. "Ken, that old jalopy of yours is almost as easy to drive as Dad's tractor. It's a good thing, though, that the sheriff didn't ask Jay last night on the phone how we got down to Payrock. It would be just like old Law-and-Order McKenney to fine me for not being old enough to have a driver's license when I was saving somebody's life."

"Jay," Ken said, "when you called the sheriff to send

the ambulance, did you think to ask him if he's had any news from Texas?"

"Jeepers! I haven't had a chance to tell you," Jay exclaimed. "I told Bert what Ashy said—that the man with the box was living in the Crater all winter and skipped out a couple of weeks ago. Bert said it was all news to him. The reward offer hasn't been canceled or claimed. But Grandma said we're nuts for believing Ashy. She said Ashy heard about the reward, and he was going into the Crater to try and get the money for himself. He just thought up that story to keep us away till his leg is healed up and he can go back and make the search."

"Your grandma always did say Ashy didn't care any more for a nickel than he did for his right arm," Doc remarked.

Ken peered through his thick glasses with sudden surprise. "Maybe your grandmother is right," he said thoughtfully. "I was going to call off the search when I talk to the rest of the Squad at noon. But now I'm beginning to think we should push right on, just as if Ashy hadn't said anything."

"You mean we won't be going back home today after all?" Jay asked him eagerly.

"Is there any reason why you can't stay over?" Ken asked in return. "We had planned to stay on through Decoration Day."

"Nuts, I thought you would be calling the hunt off, so I told Grandma to expect us this afternoon," Jay answered.

"Hurry up, run after those ambulance guys," Doc said. "Tell them to leave word at the store you're not coming home."

Jay dashed off down the trail with Benzy at his heels. The men had not gone far, and they promised to pass the message on to Grandma.

"One thing we didn't think of," Jay said to Ken as he came puffing back to Ashy's cabin. "I guess it will be all right if Benzy goes to the Crater with us, won't it?"

"I honestly don't like the idea," Ken answered. "But if you think you can get him down the chute and up again, I guess it's all right."

"Oh, he's gone worse places than that," Jay said. "Besides, there's nothing we can do about it now. He'll follow us, anyway."

The boys got their packs ready, and Ken closed the door to Ashy's cabin. "The old fellow must have been in a lot of pain this morning," Ken said. "See what he forgot? He

went off in the ambulance and left the key to his padlock here with me."

"You can send it to him in the hospital," Jay said. "Let's go."

It was nearly noon by the time they reached Granny's Wart. As they waited for the last minutes to tick away before the two walkie-talkies would be in touch with each other, Jay and Doc stood on the Divide and looked silently down. Below them lay the enormous, almost circular area that was called Devil's Crater. No place that they had ever seen was so nearly surrounded by impossible cliffs— and no place was so wild and untouched by man. The nearest road was more than twenty-five miles from the mouth of the Crater, and not even a horse trail led into it. From where they stood, they could look almost straight down at Devil's Lake, just inside the mouth of the Crater. At this distance, it looked like a flake of mica dropped down in the bottom of the valley. Around it the spruce forest crowded, black and thick. Two creeks fed the lake, and along each of them were bands of light green that showed where dense stands of aspen grew. Streaks of the green cut back into the spruce at many points, where tongues of forest fires had long ago licked into the evergreens, and aspen had grown up to take their place.

"One-oh-five to one-oh six." The sound of Ken's voice calling the Rescue Squad below broke into the boys' awed inspection of the Crater. Ken reported the successful rescue of Ashy. Then he said, "We are going down to inspect a cabin reputedly occupied by the prospector. You keep a search line stretched across the exit to the Crater and work upstream. Make camp at six o'clock. We probably won't rendezvous with you for the camp tonight. But stand by for a call at six p.m. Meanwhile, we'll work down the creek closest to us, looking for the cabin."

Jay was surprised by this conversation. "Do you really think there's a cabin down there?" he asked after Ken signed off.

"I don't think anything," Ken answered. "Maybe the old man was making the whole story up. But the way he talked last night when you were gone, I can't help thinking there is a cabin. Ashy was half out of his mind with pain. He babbled quite a lot, so it's hard to tell what was true and what wasn't. But the clue is worth checking on, and it might save us a lot of work."

The trip down the chute was easy. Even Benzy made it most of the way without having to be lifted over tough spots.

Jay felt more and more glad to have the warm, tireless presence of his underslung "pedigreed Indian gopher hound." The Crater itself was the most forbidding sight he had seen in all his years near the Continental Divide. And the closer they came to the actual search for a man who might be dead, the less enthusiastic he felt about the whole venture. It was a real relief to watch Benzy scramble yipping after a cony, or to have him come and put his head in Jay's lap as they rested.

As soon as they were out of the chute and below timberline, the going became slower. Nowhere on the eastern slope did the spruce grow so high and so thick, Jay thought to himself, while he struggled over one fallen trunk after another. Although it was still early afternoon, deep dusk surrounded the three as they headed through the woods toward the creek on which Ashy had said the cabin stood.

But at last they came out of the spruce and into a tangle of aspens. Here it was lighter, and they made better time. At one point they stood in direct sunlight.

"Well, what do you know!" Doc exclaimed. "There's beavers here."

All around them stood pointed stumps where beaver teeth had gnawed a whole section of the grove. A hundred yards farther on, they came in sight of a pond.

"We want to make sure we cover this whole creek," Ken said. "So we'll follow it up to timberline first. Then, if you haven't found a cabin, we'll double back and search both sides until we get to the lake. You two guys go up this side. I'll cross that beaver dam and search the far side."

But Doc had already started toward the dam while Ken was talking. "Hey, fellows," he called. "There's something here that might be a trail!"

A faint line of broken limbs and bark that had been scratched off the tops of fallen logs led back from the creek into the woods.

"Looks like somebody has gone through here several times. Let's have a look along it before we head up toward timberline," Jay suggested.

"Okay. But we won't go far," Ken said.

The trail led them past two more small beaver ponds. All of a sudden Benzy, who was just ahead, began a furious yipping. He had been doing that off and on all day, so none of the three thought anything of it. Then Doc cried, "Hey, the pooch is after a little beaver!"

Benzy had flushed the half-grown animal out of the woods at the right of the trail. Now it was waddling clumsily as fast as it could across the trail toward the safety of water.

Jay and Ken watched in amusement, but Doc said, "By golly, I think that was a black beaver. I never saw one so dark, except those we helped Van plant over on the Middle Fork!"

"Wait till we tell Van about this!" said Jay.

"Say," Doc said, "can't you guys take Benzy off and look for the cabin? Let me wait here and make sure if they are black ones."

"It's never good to divide a party up," Ken answered. "You know that."

"Hold on a minute," Jay cried. "Do you see what I see?" He pointed ahead through the trees. Without a word the three of them pushed on for a closer look. No question about it. They had found a small log cabin, just as Ashy said they would.

Ken took the lead, and as they came close to the cabin, he called out, "Hello! Hello! Anybody home?"

There was no answer. Curiously the boys looked at the windowless walls of the little structure. The door, made of heavy, handhewn spruce planks, was held shut with a piece of string. Ken knocked on the door.

"You sure are polite, Ken," Doc said. "Couldn't be anybody in there with the door tied shut from the outside the way it is."

Ken gave one of his rare chuckles and opened the door. It was almost impossible to see through the gloom inside. "Get out a flashlight," he said.

Jay swung off his pack. In another moment the beam of the electric torch played over the bare interior. Along one wall lay a thick heap of fairly fresh spruce boughs that had obviously been used for a mattress. On the small sheet-iron stove sat a frying pan and a pot. In one corner was a heap of split firewood and beside it a block that had been used as a stool. On the block sat a covered lard pail. As far as they could see there was nothing else in the room except a tin cup that hung from a nail in the wall.

"Ashy sure was right," Doc said. "The crazy man's been living here. Those spruce boughs are fairly fresh, too. Maybe he did just leave, the way Ashy said."

Jay idly lifted the lard bucket. It rattled, so he pried the top off. Inside were a dozen candles, salt, pepper, sugar, and a little flour. "It looks as if the guy intends to come back," Jay said. "Maybe he's just gone out to get some fresh supplies."

"Maybe we better not be in here when he comes back, either," Doc said uneasily. "There's no telling what that guy will do."

Ken was saying nothing. He was obviously puzzled.

Jay was puzzled, too. This was no old, abandoned miner's shack of the kind he was used to on the eastern slope. The cabin was new—not more than a year old, he would say. He stood in the door and peered out. The space in front of the cabin didn't look trampled and used, the way he thought it would look if a man had lived there all winter long. He walked all around the outside of the little house. Between two rocks nearby lay a small heap of tin cans. They weren't badly rusted, and he felt sure nobody could have lived for very long on the small amount of food that had been in the cans.

But then, he thought, the cans would have been mighty heavy to lug in. The wild idea crossed his mind that the crazy guy might have lived on food pills—the kind the Rescue Squad carried with them for emergencies. He laughed at himself and pushed past Ken and Doc who were now outside looking around, too.

"I don't get this layout, do you?" Jay said to the others, then he went into the cabin again. He pushed the door shut, wondering what it would be like to live cooped up in this windowless room for a whole long winter. The dark of it all gave him the creeps. A few cracks around the door let in rays of the late afternoon sunlight, but the gloom was deep and almost frightening.

Jay flashed on his light quickly, and it picked up something that the door had hidden when it was open—an ax. Beside it stood a small greasy-looking bottle.

"Here's an ax, Ken," Jay called. "If we want to camp here, it'll come in handy."

Jay picked up the bottle, shook it, found it was almost empty, set it down, and then hurried out into the sunlight.

"I think we can put up here for the night," Ken was saying. "I can climb that knob of rock over here. That may help reception when we make our six o'clock call to the others. Meanwhile we can scour around the camp here and see if we can figure out anything. Maybe the fellows down below have picked up some sign of the prospector's trail by now, if he went out."

Jay's hands felt greasy after touching the bottle inside the cabin. He rubbed his fingers uncomfortably, and suddenly he realized that an odd, strong smell was clinging to them. At the same time a picture crossed his mind. He saw Van setting the beaver trap last August.

"Doc!" Jay exclaimed. "Smell this." He pushed his finger tips up close to Doc's surprised face.

"Whew! Take it away!" Doc snorted.

"Does that remind you of anything?" Jay asked.

"Reminds me it's Sunday night and you need a bath," Doc answered.

"Quit kidding. Think where you've smelled that before," Jay said. "Doesn't it remind you of the bait that Van put in the beaver traps when we went with him that time last summer?"

"Say, it does, kind of," Doc answered. "Let me smell it again. It does! It stinks just as bad. Where did you get it?"

"There's a bottle of it in the cabin," Jay said.

"You better sleep inside with the door closed tonight," Doc said. "Otherwise you'll have a beaver waking you up. Remember that swanky dame with the perfume?"

The two boys burst out laughing at the memory of Mrs. Jerrold George III and the sun-bathers. Benzy wiggled over in front of them and looked up at Jay as if he, too, wanted to be in on the fun. The sudden laughter was a kind of relief that broke the somber silence of the forest and freed them from the oppressive darkness of the tiny cabin.

"What's got into you fellows?" Ken asked. "Has the altitude affected you?"

"Smell Jay," Doc howled and gasped for breath.

With complete seriousness, Ken did as requested. Then he wrinkled his sunburned face in disgust. "You smell like rotten old fish," he said.

"That's not all," Jay said. "I smell like licorice and castor and fancy perfume, too. Do you know what it is? Beaver bait."

"Where did it come from?" Ken asked.

Jay told him and then explained why they were laughing. But Ken didn't smile. "I suppose the prospector was trapping beaver. Isn't that illegal?"

"Sure, nobody is allowed to do it except official state trappers," Doc said. "Maybe one of Van's men has this cabin—not the crazy man at all."

For some time the three of them sat on a log and spun theories. They had passed a series of beaver dams. This would be a good place for trapping. On the other hand, beavers did more good than harm in this kind of wild country, so why should Van send trappers here? But if it was really a black beaver that Doc saw, perhaps the state men were taking them out to transplant elsewhere.

"Well, I can find out if they're black," Doc said. "Van showed us what to do if we wanted to see beavers in a hurry. Let's just go down and tear a hole in one of the dams. The little rascals will come running to patch it up. This is the best time of day for it, too. Just before sundown."

"Aw, you just want to watch beavers," Jay said, smiling. "Tearing a hole in a dam is a lot of work."

"Maybe," Doc answered. "Can I, Ken?"

"I guess so," Ken answered. "We don't have anything much to do except wait till six o'clock."

"Look, Ken, do us a favor, will you?" Doc said. "You hold Benzy on a rope while we're out there. He'd scare the beavers so we couldn't see anything."

With one of his rare flashes of humor, Ken said, "Well, this is the first time I ever heard of walking a dog on a leash in the wilderness." But in a minute he was off casually poking around the woods, holding Benzy at the end of a piece of nylon cord, looking as silly and out of place as he felt.

Jay and Doc made quick work of tearing an opening in the dam. They stood back as the torrent of water poured through the gap. Then they crouched as close to the hole as they could and waited. Not many minutes passed before the surface of the pond began to drop a little.

"Look! It's working," Doc whispered, pointing to a ripple in the water near the beaver lodge. The beaver in the lodge had discovered that the water level was dropping and had come out to investigate. Soon a big animal, followed by a small one, was nosing around the break in the dam. A quick look at the hole, and the two disappeared under the water. Then the big fellow came back, swimming heavily as he pulled a large branch from the storage pile he kept under water for food. As he wrestled to place the branch across the opening, he climbed out on the dam. And he was as black as any beaver could be!

The boys ran back to the cabin to tell the news. They saw Ken coming toward them out of the woods, still holding Benzy dutifully on the rope. The little dog had something in his mouth.

"They *are* black," Doc called. "Will Van want to hear this!"

"Here, Benzy," Jay called. "You can let him go now, Ken."

Ken let go of the rope. Benzy ran up to Jay and as usual

dropped his treasure at his master's feet.

"That's a beaver head!" Doc cried. "Where did he get it, Ken?"

"There is a big crack in the rock back there a way," Ken answered. "It seems to be full of bones and refuse."

"Does this stink!" said Jay, as he bent down to inspect the skull. It still had hair on it.

Doc held his nose and leaned over to take a close look. "Black!" he shouted excitedly. "The crazy man has been killing black beaver! Van's men always trap them alive."

Ken had been looking thoughtful. "Van may be glad for the information," he said, "but we still have our own job to do. Let's go up on that knob now. It will soon be six o'clock."

No sooner had Ken established contact with the main group of searchers than Jay and Doc saw he was deeply excited about something. He didn't even try to tell about their own discovery of the cabin and the evidence of poaching. Finally he said, "Okay. A good job. You got your picture all right, didn't you? See you tomorrow night. We'll go back out the way we came in."

"What's up? Why didn't you tell them about the cabin and stuff?" Jay protested.

"They found the prospector's body," Ken said. "He's been dead all winter. Apparently he was caught in the first heavy blizzard of the season when he was trying to get up out of the Crater."

## CHAPTER 22 ... Benzy, the Sleuth

"I leave it to you fellows," Ken said. "We can hike on to the car and get soaking wet. Or we can duck into Ashy's cabin and wait for the rain to blow over. No telling how long that will be. Which do you want to do?"

"What's the rush?" Doc said. "Let's stay dry, as long as you've got Ashy's key. We did him a big favor, and now he can do us one."

The rain started to come down hard as they stood outside Ashy's door, near his big pile of rusty old scrap metal.

"Okay by me to stay," Jay said.

They soon had a fire in the old man's cook stove and made hot soup from packages of dried powder they carried in their packs. A real sense of coziness and security soon filled the warm room, while rain came down in torrents outside. They had all talked themselves out about yesterday's events and now they ate in silence. Jay put a bowl of soup aside to cool, then set it on the immaculately clean floor.

"Here, Benzy dog," he said. "Here you are. But be careful not to splash it on the floor. Ashy keeps this place clean."

There was a rustle under Ashy's bunk, and Benzy appeared with something in his mouth.

"Oh, gosh, what you got now?" Jay scolded. Then he jumped up, and a cold blow of fear struck him in the pit of his stomach. "Benzy! Benzy!" he whispered in a tense voice. "Easy. Let Jay have it, boy." With no sudden motion to frighten the dog, he stretched out his hand to receive what Benzy was carrying.

With his other hand, Jay caught Benzy by the collar. "Doc, you throw him out. I don't care if he does get wet. Look what he's found! Dynamite!"

"Dynamite!" Doc and Ken both exclaimed at once.

"Where did the dog get it?" Ken asked.

"Right under you—under the bunk," Jay told him. "If there's any more, I sure don't want Benzy to get at it. There might be caps in there, too. If he should bite into one of them he might blow us all sky high."

When the dog was outside, Jay got down on the floor and searched under the bunk. There he found a small wooden box with more sticks of dynamite, about the thickness of a candle and a bit longer, each one wrapped in heavy, yellowish oiled paper. Beside the box was a coil of white fuse. The caps, Jay discovered with relief, were in a tightly capped tin box.

"They say this stuff is safe to leave around, but it scares the dickens out of me," Jay said. "Grandma's told me about too many mine accidents."

"What do you suppose Ashy's doing with dynamite, anyway?" Doc asked.

"Doesn't he own this mine here?" Ken asked.

"Yeah," Jay answered. He turned toward the window and looked at Ashy's scrap heap. The sudden downpour had let up, and there was Benzy nosing around the pile of old iron. "Yeah, Ashy owns the mine, but he never worked inside it a day in his life. Grandma says he's always hated the idea of going underground. He's been waiting for the price of ore to go high enough so that it will pay him to get some real miners in here to do the digging for him."

"Then what in the world—" Ken mused.

A scratching at the door interrupted his question. Jay tried to pay no attention to Benzy. It wouldn't hurt the pooch to stay out a little longer. But the scratching continued, and Jay finally said, "I'm going to let him in and tie him up so he can't get near the dynamite."

"Okay, but watch out he doesn't slip between your legs," Ken said. He shifted his feet, ready, if necessary, to keep Benzy from running under the bunk again.

Jay opened the door just wide enough to get his arm out, grabbed Benzy's collar and pulled him in. With a mighty shake of his short-haired little frame, the dog expressed delight at being indoors. Water sprayed all over Jay. Then Benzy dropped something at Jay's feet.

"You can't even stop stealing in bad weather, can you?" Jay said, fastening the cord he had taken from his pack. "I'm going to send you to a psychiatrist to see what's wrong with you. Hey, Ken, have they got any courses in college that tell what makes you go stealing just for the fun of it?"

"What did he swipe this time?" Doc asked.

"Something he took off of Ashy's scrap heap," Jay answered. He picked up a small, leathery object to which a shiny piece of metal was sticking and tossed it to Doc.

"Holy smoke! Do you know what this is?" Doc asked. "It's a beaver ear—with one of those tags in it that Van uses to keep track of his transplants! Where do you suppose Ashy got it?"

"We can find out where it came from, because Van's got a record of the numbers on it in his F.B.I. file," Jay answered.

"Jeepers, there isn't any piece of metal too small for that old guy to save, is there?" Doc asked wonderingly.

"Keep still. I'm thinking," Jay answered. Suddenly a lot of unrelated things had begun to fall into place in Jay's mind. Could it be that Ashy was poaching beaver—both in Devil's Crater and on the Middle Fork? Ashy knew all about the little cabin in the Crater. Somebody was poaching there. Somebody kept the little cabin as neat as Ashy kept this place. Ashy had tried to prevent their going down into the Crater. Maybe he was afraid they would somehow find out about the poaching. Could he have been stealing black beavers for several years? He lived right here close to the preserve on Middle Fork. He might even have planted brown beavers in place of the black ones he took out of the preserve. But Jay couldn't imagine why the old man would go to all that trouble.

"There's something fishy about this beaver business," Jay said after a minute. "I think we ought to look around this place a little."

"I think we ought to head for home," Ken said. "We have no right to search another man's property. You should tell Van Hollister and let him handle the matter."

Jay knew that Ken was right. "I'm not going to break into anything. I just want to have a look-see outside." Taking Benzy with him, he went out. In all the times he had passed Ashy's place he had never been around behind the cabin. Not far away was the black opening that marked the mine tunnel. Ashy wouldn't go in there for love nor money. There was nothing else in sight except a lean-to at the back side of the cabin. An old-fashioned latch held the lean-to door shut. Jay tried it and the door swung open. There, before his eyes, three live-traps for beaver hung from the wall.

Benzy nuzzled up against Jay's leg. "Benzy, you thieving, low-down, pedigreed Indian gopher hound," Jay said, "I'm beginning to think you've got the jinx of Payrock Canyon on the run."

# CHAPTER 23 ... "Hiking Hawkshaws"

Jay and Doc jumped out of the Martins' car which had brought them up to Payrock after school on Friday afternoon. They raced along the platform in front of the store, and Jay yelled, "Hey, Grandma! Have you seen the paper?"

"Goodness, gracious!" Grandma exclaimed. "Of course I haven't seen the paper. The mail just came."

Jay slapped down that day's copy of the Denver *Gazette* on the counter. "Get your glasses, Grandma, quick," he said, "and read this."

Even without her glasses Grandma could read the big headline on the front page which Jay was pointing to:

## HIKING HAWKSHAWS JOLT JINX

"Mercy upon us, have you gone and scared away some more tourists with your jinx ideas?" she scolded. "Why don't they write the kind of headlines that a body can understand, anyway?"

Impatiently, Jay got the old lady's glasses from their regular spot in front of the bottles of sunburn lotion on the shelf and poked them at her nose. "Come on, read it," he implored.

As Grandma adjusted the spectacles, she said, "I don't suppose you remembered to do as I said and phone the hospital to find out how bad Ashy was hurt."

"Read the story. It tells everything," Doc put in.

"Well, now, let's see." Grandma began to read. " 'The mystery of the jinx of Payrock Canyon, which was first reported in these columns last August, has been solved by a resolute group of young mountaineers belonging to the Search and Rescue Squad of Fremont. Our readers will recall that a series of frightening events have driven tourists away from the mountain recreation area around Payrock. Now, the 'Gazette' is able to report exclusively that the cause of all these events has been found, and we have placed evidence in the hands of District Attorney James Dillworth which has brought about the arrest of a mountain character, S. C. Ashforth, widely known as "Ashy." Charges against the aged eccentric include large-scale illegal trapping of beaver, poaching on the state's treasured mountain sheep preserve, attempted atrocious assault, and malicious mischief.' "

Grandma paused. "My gracious!" she said. "I always knew Ashy was an ornery old cuss, but I don't believe a word of this. It sounds just like newspaper talk."

"Go on. Keep reading," Jay said cheerily.

" 'A warrant for the arrest of a prominent Eastern businessman, Jerrold George III, who owns the Sky High Ranch near Payrock, has also been issued. According to evidence collected by the 'Gazette,' George acted as receiver of high-grade black beaver pelts illegally trapped by Ashforth.' "

Grandma stared at Jay. "Aren't you ashamed of yourself making up stories like this?" she said sternly. "Jason Himrod, you're going to get into trouble."

Both Jay and Doc tried to control giggles. "Go on, Grandma."

" 'In addition, an employee of the Mountain States Fur and Taxidermy Company, Incorporated, is charged with conspiracy to defraud the State of Colorado and also with breaking various provisions of the State game laws. Allegedly, this employee arranged for the illicit beaver pelts to be made into ladies' coats valued at a fabulous price, but which were presented as gifts by George to the wives of various business associates.' "

Grandma put the paper down firmly. "I can't read that kind of stuff," she said. "You boys had better tell me what it's all about."

"I'll start at the beginning, Grandma," Jay said. "Last week end Benzy and Doc and Ken and I found a lot of clues, but I didn't want to talk to you about them till I was sure."

"Better talk to me than to that reporter," Grandma snapped.

"You remember I told you how the Squad found the body of the man with the box," Jay went on. "Well, Tuesday the papers all printed the story. But they didn't give the Rescue Squad hardly any credit at all! Every single one of the reporters went on and on about Sheriff Bert McKenney says this, Sheriff McKenney says that, and then at the very end, some of them said the Squad found the body. It made me so mad, I called up the 'Gazette' reporter to see if he wouldn't write the real story of what had happened. While I was telling him about the search, I mentioned some other things that we'd found out."

Grandma nodded. "Well, Bert McKenney always was

one to blow his own horn. But why didn't you talk to Van Hollister if you thought there was poaching?" Grandma wanted to know.

"I tried, but he was away for three days," Jay answered. "Anyway, the reporter talked to Van, and he talked to Ashy, too. That's how he got most of the story."

"Now don't tell me Ashy told anybody anything," Grandma said. "That old grouch wouldn't give you the time of day, let alone say he was a criminal and get himself arrested."

"The reporter got him to talk, just the same," Doc put in. "Honest, you have to believe Jay. We even know how he made Ashy confess."

"How?" Grandma asked skeptically.

"The reporter scared him into thinking he'd be arrested for murdering the man with the box," Jay said. "He pointed out that Ashy was probably the last one to see the man alive, and that Ashy kept claiming he knew so much about the fellow. Ashy blamed the man for everything bad that happened. The reporter just guessed that Ashy himself caused all of the troubles but was trying to cover it up by blaming somebody else. He told Ashy any jury would believe he wanted to get rid of the man with the box."

"Now don't tell me there's murder in this, too," Grandma said.

"I'm *not* saying it," Jay protested. "The prospector was just a darn fool for hiking in the mountains alone. He froze to death. But the reporter used the idea of murder to scare a real confession out of Ashy. Wait till you hear what Ashy told! For three years Ashy has been stealing the black beavers that Van planted in the hanging valley on the Middle Fork. Ashy always put other beavers in their place, because he thought that was a way to avoid suspicion. Then Ashy got Mr. George to fly the live black beavers in his plane over to Devil's Lake. Ashy let them out above there, along the creek, and they started a whole colony of black ones. They multiplied like crazy. This year he harvested more than a hundred pelts and sold them to Mr. George. You know, Mr. George is an awful fancy guy, and he wanted black beaver coats to give away so he could act like a big shot, because there aren't very many coats like that in the world."

"Of all the nonsense," Grandma said. "Black beaver isn't any warmer than brown beaver."

Jay went on to explain that Mr. George also liked to pretend he was a big game hunter. So he paid Ashy to shoot some old bighorn rams. He got their heads stuffed and mounted at the same place where he had the beaver pelts fixed up. Ashy had been the one who moved the mountain sheep's salt last summer. He did this so the sheep would stay close to where he lived and he wouldn't have trouble hunting them. Then, when the open season on bighorn sheep was declared, Ashy thought he was darned lucky. He got himself a license and figured he could use it to account for one of the rams he had already killed.

Grandma listened, shaking her head. "But none of this explains the jinx business you keep talking about, Jay," she said.

"That's easy," Jay answered. "Ashy had fixed things so that he could get thousands of dollars' worth of beaver pelts every year. He had a fine hideaway over there in Devil's Crater, because almost nobody ever goes to the place. By this spring, he had enough of the black ones in the Crater so that they would keep themselves going. The ones that Van brought to Middle Fork were just an extra bonus. But Ashy wanted to discourage Van, so that the Game and Fish Department men wouldn't be nosing around. That was why he did all of his jinxing. He wanted to scare just *everybody* away from his part of the mountains. He was going to keep on scaring them, too."

All this seemed so plain to Jay now that he couldn't imagine why he hadn't seen through Ashy's scheme a long time ago. Take the rock slide the night they rescued the red-headed twins. Ashy had pretended to go home, and then he climbed up on the ridge above the trail and rolled a big boulder down in the direction of the rescue party. He had started the other landslide when Van's men were carrying the salt for the sheep back to where it belonged. He had used a charge of dynamite to make that slide. He had used more dynamite to blow up the uranium prospector's cabin. The prospector had really made Ashy worry, because he went all over the place poking into things. Ashy even thought the fellow might stay around and spy on him.

When the boys from Camp Wapiti started hiking up in the mountains, Ashy stampeded the cattle to scare them away. Then he stampeded a herd through the camp. He wanted to drive the camp clear away, and he had succeeded. The camp owner had decided not to return to Wapiti this year. At the same time, Ashy thought he would frighten Mr. Martin into moving his cattle to another range—and he had succeeded in that, too, at least for last year. It was a slick trick, of course, when he ran two steers over a cliff and then brought in their ears as if he were doing Mr. Martin a favor to warn him about the "crazy man."

A great light dawned on Grandma. "So the prospector wasn't crazy at all?" she asked.

"No, he just didn't have very good sense. Ken said a lot of these uranium prospectors act mysterious, because they want to find ore and stake out their claims before anybody else does. He took chances every time he went out alone, and finally he took one chance too many."

"All right," Grandma said with a twinkle in her eyes. "What about those patches of aspen trees turning brown and dying all around here? I suppose Ashy jinxed them, too?"

Doc laughed. "No, that's one thing he didn't have anything to do with. My science teacher explained it. You remember there was a warm spell February before last? It got so warm that sap began to rise in the trees. Then a sudden cold snap came on. The cold hit some spots worse than others because of the way the wind was blowing. It just froze the sap all of a sudden in those trees. They swelled up and died. Some of them started to grow leaves in the spring, but they were too far gone to succeed."

"Well, Jay," Grandma said, "it looks as if this summer

you'll be able to give me a little help around here, instead of running off to rescue folks who have been jinxed or something."

"Uh-oh!" Doc said. "I'm afraid you're wrong, Mrs. Himrod. You read the end of that story in the paper."

Grandma put on her glasses again and read the paragraph Doc pointed to. " 'The key figures in solving this mystery of the jinx of Payrock Canyon were Jason Himrod and Hallet ("Doc") Martin, two members of the sophomore class at Fremont High School. Not only did they turn up the main clues that led to the apprehension of Ashforth and George, but they participated heroically in several difficult mountain rescues. Ironically, it was these two youths, together with Kenneth Schultz, student at Fremont College, who saved the life of Ashforth himself just last week. In recognition of the outstanding ability and service of Himrod and Martin, the Search and Rescue Squad this week at a special meeting made the two boys full members, thus breaking the Squad's long-standing precedent of admitting only people of college age.' "

In spite of himself, a lump came into Jay's throat as he heard Grandma reading out the words of praise. Then, with a husky voice, he said to Doc, "I been meaning to tell you something. I fixed it all up with Ken about that crazy toboggan ride you got last fall. I said I was to blame because I dropped the rope on purpose. It sure was swell of him to let me into the Rescue Squad after that."

Just then Benzy scratched at the door. Doc opened it, and the dog rushed to Jay, whom he hadn't seen for a week. His yellow body wiggled all over as he stood on his hind legs and licked Jay's hand.

"Hello, you low-down, thieving, pedigreed Indian gopher hound," Jay said. "For once you haven't stolen anything. And you know what—if it hadn't been for you, we never would have found the jinxer of Payrock Canyon."

# Whitman
# CLASSICS

Five Little Peppers Midway

Mrs. Wiggs of the
　　Cabbage Patch

Fifty Famous Fairy Tales

Eight Cousins

Little Women

Black Beauty

Five Little Peppers and
　　How They Grew

Treasure Island

Heidi

The Call of the Wild

Tom Sawyer

Beautiful Joe

Adventures of Sherlock Holmes

Little Lame Prince

Here are some of the best-loved stories of all time.
Delightful ... intriguing ... never-to-be-forgotten
tales that you will read again and again. Start
your own home library of WHITMAN CLASSICS
so that you'll always have exciting books at your
finger tips.

# Whitman ADVENTURE and MYSTERY Books

## Adventure Stories for GIRLS and BOYS...

### TIMBER TRAIL RIDERS
The Long Trail North
The Texas Tenderfoot
The Luck of Black Diamond
Mystery of the Hollywood Horse
The Mysterious Dude

### POWER BOYS SERIES
The Haunted Skyscraper
The Flying Skeleton

### DONNA PARKER
In Hollywood
At Cherrydale
Special Agent
On Her Own
A Spring to Remember
Mystery at Arawak
Takes a Giant Step

### TROY NESBIT SERIES
Sand Dune Pony
Diamond Cave Mystery
Indian Mummy Mystery
Mystery at Rustlers' Fort

## New Stories About Your Television Favorites...

### Dr. Kildare
Assigned to Trouble
The Magic Key

### Janet Lennon at Camp Calamity

### Walt Disney's Annette
Mystery at Smugglers' Cove
Desert Inn Mystery
Sierra Summer
Mystery at Moonstone Bay
Mystery at Medicine Wheel

### Combat! The Counterattack

### The Beverly Hillbillies

### Lassie
Secret of the Summer
Forbidden Valley
Mystery at Blackberry Bog

### Lucy and the Madcap Mystery

### Patty Duke and Mystery Mansion

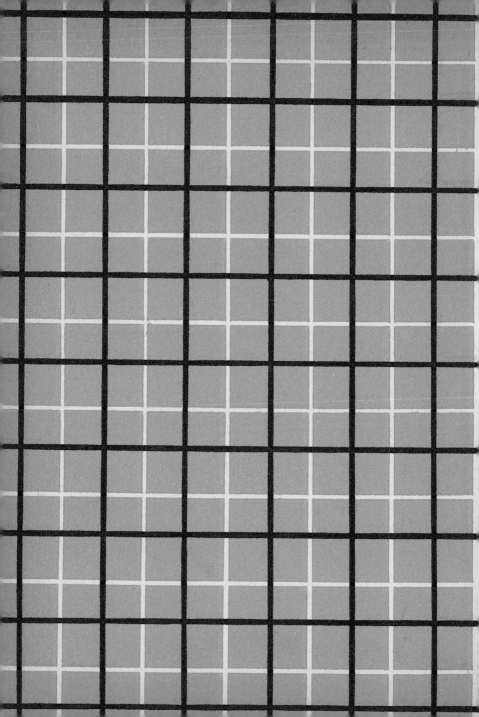